DOUBLE
DiGiT

To Violette,

DOUBLE DIGIT

By Annabel Monaghan

Enjoy!

Annabel Monaghan

Houghton Mifflin Harcourt
Boston New York

www.hmhco.com

The text of this book is set in Apollo MT.

The Library of Congress has cataloged the hardcover edition as follows:
Monaghan, Annabel.
Double Digit / Annabel Monaghan.
p. cm.
Summary: "Digit attends MIT, where she hopes to lead a normal life.
But Jonas Furnis, the ecoterrorist she foiled before, knows where she is,
and he's gunning for her" —Provided by publisher.
[1. Interpersonal relations—Fiction. 2. Universities and colleges—Fiction. 3.
Computer hackers—Fiction. 4. Ecoterrorism—Fiction. 5. Terrorism—Fiction.
6. Adventure and adventurers—Fiction. 7. Massachusetts Institute of
Technology—Fiction.] I. Title.
PZ7.M73649Dou 2014
[Fic]—dc23
2013004153

ISBN: 978-0-544-10577-5 hardcover
ISBN: 978-0-544-33620-9 paperback

Manufactured in the United States of America
DOC 10 9 8 7 6 5 4 3 2 1

4500508021

For my dad, Charles Schwedes, code master

If people do not believe that mathematics is simple, it is only because they do not realize how complicated life is.

— JOHN VON NEUMANN

WHAT COULD POSSIBLY GO WRONG?

MY NEW FAVORITE BUMPER STICKER: WHAT COULD POSSIBLY GO WRONG? It's the question that the completely clueless ask when standing in the middle of their perfect happy ending. And what follows is usually a movie-scale epic disaster. It would be the ideal bumper sticker for the back of my car, but I just might wait and have it put on my tombstone someday. I saw it on a Volkswagen in the LAX parking lot as I was leaving for MIT. I think I'm going to have to start paying better attention to omens.

It's funny to think that I spent the first eighteen years of my life putting things in perfect order: math problems, number sequences, puzzles. I'd think them into orderly submission and then revel in the crisp solution. Even the bumper stickers that cover the four walls of my bedroom are lined up at perfect right angles. This is my defining characteristic, this preoccupation with order. Which is why it's really hilarious-slash-tragic that I never focused on all the loose ends.

I mean, maybe it was the whole near-death thing and the falling-in-love thing that blurred me a little. I was in such a rush to get to the romantic finale that I wanted my story to wrap up nice and neat: The bad guys are caught and the young lovers are headed off to Hawaii for a little rest and relaxation. *What could possibly go wrong?*

Seriously? It turns out that 1) there are plenty of un-caught other, even worse bad guys out there, and 2) I have parents who frown on me jetting off for a pre-honeymoon honeymoon with my new boyfriend. Of course, I've listed these outcomes in reverse order of tragedy.

The truth is that life isn't nice and neat. At least mine isn't. You never know what or who is waiting around the corner. Sometimes it's a guy with a knife; sometimes it's a casually placed kiss. The bottom line is that none of it was part of my plan.

And I should have known better. You don't get yourself nose-deep in trouble, hunted by a crazy bunch of terrorists, and then walk away with a new attitude and a cute boyfriend. This isn't a sitcom, and the credits never rolled on the whole story. I should have known trouble would follow me. And that you shouldn't go ahead and mess with national security just because you can. Really, *what could possibly go wrong?*

IF YOU KNEW MY FAMILY, YOU'D UNDERSTAND

MY SECOND (IGNORED) OMEN WAS THE human torch I'd been assigned as a roommate. I should have known she was going to be the match that got the whole fire blazing. When my parents and I got to my dorm on the first day of freshman orientation, she was already there. She is about five foot ten and impossibly skinny with bright red hair, cut short and spiked straight up. I had to pause a few beats at the sight of her. "Hi, are you Farrah? I'm Tiki."

She is the most perfectly named person I have ever known.

She is from Virginia, and her parents were driving back that night. Anxious to beat the traffic, they made the obligatory trip to Bed Bath & Beyond and then hit the road. My parents seemed to have all the time in the world. In fact, I was scared to ask when their return flight left. Not what time, but more like what day.

Not that there's anything really wrong with my parents. It's just that I was hoping to slip quietly into college, blending in, in a low-key sort of way. And my mom did not blend in, especially in Massachusetts. She wore white leggings (there are only six people on earth who can get away with wearing white leggings — my mom is one of them) and a turquoise tunic with sequins along the cuffs that caught the light as she gestured. She was way too bright for New England and made me feel like I was being followed by an oddly beautiful neon sign. My dad, on the other hand, blended beautifully. All tweed and khaki, in a rainbow of beige. He seemed as if we could have just happened upon him at MIT: a quietly friendly math professor whose mind was chewing on something that no one but me would understand.

"Girls, those metal blinds are not going to do. What do you say we take a trip into Boston and hit the Marimekko store and see what we can find?" My mom clapped her hands together like a kindergarten teacher calling us all onto the rug for circle time. When we didn't move, she pressed on. "Tiki, this is in your best interest. If we don't do a little decorating fast, she's going to cover these walls in bumper stickers. Now, we don't want that, do we?"

"I brought posters?" Tiki was proceeding with caution, not knowing exactly how to handle my mom's enthusiasm.

"Mom, we've got it. We'll be fine. How about Tiki and I get settled in, and we can all, including you, talk about decorating at parents' weekend in October?"

I'd just stuck a pin in her. "Fine. And in October you give me four hours in the Copley Place mall?"

"Three."

"Deal."

Finally, they left. Tiki and I were both excited and nervous, sizing each other up. Tiki sat cross-legged and perfectly balanced on a desk chair, watching me. She had a way of moving her long body and slowly unfolding her limbs that reminded me of a cartoon character. "Farrah? Is there another name for you? I mean, I'm just not feeling it. Tiki and Farrah rock MIT? It doesn't seem right."

I looked down at my boots. They needed to be resoled and maybe polished. I'd worn them just about every day since the ninth grade, and I'm more and more sure as time goes by that they have magical powers. It was my goal to be as comfortable in every part of my life as I was in those boots. "Yeah, in middle school they called me Digit because I like math." And so it was out there, on day one: Digit.

"Awesome. Tiki and Digit. This is going to be epic."

4

She continued unpacking her things. She took the bed closer to the window and covered it with a turquoise bedspread, embroidered with a giant peacock. There was going to be nothing subtle about Tiki.

"You mind if I hang these?" She unrolled two posters, both prints of works by Adam Ranks, a popular Los Angeles graphic artist who'd become even more popular since he'd been kidnapped three weeks before.

I sucked in a little air. "Oh. Adam Ranks, right? Have they found him?" I tried to sound casual, like a person with no personal experience with kidnapping.

"No. He's history. Two guys came to his house, tied up his wife, and took him." She dropped a poster, and I watched it roll back up on itself. I knew exactly how it felt. "They left no fingerprints; no one saw the car. The police have nothing." She picked up the poster and taped it to the wall, reasonably straight, but not nearly straight enough. "You okay?"

"Yeah, just a little surprised. I mean, I thought that was local news in L.A. You seem to know a lot about it." I walked over to retape the poster exactly straight and ran my finger across it. It was a simple geometric design of an evergreen tree, with an overlay of a sparkling poppy that seemed to be 3-D. "How does he do this?"

"He invented this special printer that creates digital prints that can be overlaid with lots of different textures. The designs are easy to make but impossible to print without his printer. His is the only one that exists. His wife has been keeping it locked away since he's been gone. She thinks someone's after the technology. Cool, right?"

"Cool." *Not cool*. This was the last thing I wanted to talk about on my first day of college. This was supposed to be a forward-moving day, and thinking about those Jonas Furnis nuts trying to kidnap me just because I'd cracked their stupid code seemed kind of counterproductive. Of course, there were good parts, like my sort-of-fun fake kidnapping by the FBI. And John. I mean, I think about that all the time. But the idea

5

of a real kidnapping and what almost happened to me were topics I'd rather leave back in Los Angeles.

Tiki unrolled the second poster and held it against the wall for my inspection. The background was a brick colonial house, overlaid with six concentric circles. But the circles must have been drawn freehand: the largest appeared to be a bit smushed and was begging to be pressed from the left a tad to get it back to 360 degrees. I reached out my hand as if I could fix it and saw Tiki staring at me.

"What are you doing?"

I thought for a minute about how far I'd come. How free I'd felt all summer just being unapologetically Digit. I took a deep breath and spit out, "They're not perfect circles. And I know this is kinda nuts, but my mind really needs them to be." I went on to explain my little unnamed disorder and how my gift for solving any math problem occasionally accelerates into hyperfocus on patterns and imperfections.

"That why you dress like that?"

I laughed and looked down at my jeans (I have four pairs, identical) and my T-shirt (I have eight in three colors). "Pretty much. Keeps my mind clear."

"Well, you're a regular Albert Einstein. Eccentric, simply dressed, but with better hair."

I smiled gratefully.

"Now that we've let your crazy out of the box, let's get this room together. I'll just hang up this one. Is it even enough for you?"

I looked again at the evergreen tree and the poppy. Neither was perfectly symmetrical, but the balance was there. The evergreen erred to the left, while the poppy erred to the right. This happens in nature all the time, and Adam Ranks understood it and had replicated it perfectly. At that moment it felt like he was speaking directly to me. Honestly, it gave me the creeps.

"I'm going to get going," Tiki announced after about an hour of unpacking. "My boyfriend, Howard, lives in a single

6

across campus, so I'll probably be spending a lot of nights there."

"You have a boyfriend already? We've been here eight hours."

Tiki laughed. "No, we've been together since high school. I was a sophomore and Howard was a junior when we first started dating. He's the reason I came here, really. I wanted to go to Brown to study art—I'm no aerospace geek. But they have an Art, Culture and Technology major here that's pretty cool. And my parents are thrilled because they think I'll become all buttoned up and eventually get a real job. Which I won't. I mean, please. But I think distance is tough on a relationship. And this thing with Howard is pretty serious, maybe the real deal. I think." There was something about the way the light left her face as she said this. It was like she wasn't buying her own story.

"I've never done the long-distance thing." Hello, or even the normal boyfriend thing, besides this summer. "But my boyfriend is moving to New York. We're going to try to visit each other and make it work." I could hear the laughter of the thousands of people before me who had said the exact same thing, only to have the whole relationship unravel during the first week of school. But it was different with John and me. We were sort of handpicked for each other. We'd figure it out.

"Where is he in school?"

"He's out of school; he's older." Her eyebrows popped up, and I laughed. "No, not like Clint Eastwood older—he's just twenty-one, but he started college early and finished in a couple of years, so this is his second year with the FBI."

"That's hot, but what's with the big rush?"

"I don't know. It's just the way he is. He has a lot to prove. He's a little worried about me running off to New York every weekend and missing college like he did. But I think I can do both. We'll just have to see how it goes."

I wasn't going to get all gooey and explain to her what it was like between John and me. How he saved my life and

7

gave up his dream job and knew me completely and embraced my craziness. When we were lying on the beach in Malibu just days before, it actually felt impossible that there would ever be a time when we wouldn't be together. "Get your education," he'd said. "It's important for you and probably for the whole world. We'll make the distance work. And when we're apart, you can cure cancer and figure out what to do with all the world's garbage. When you finish school, we can find a way to be in the same place, like normal people. I'm not going anywhere. Ever." *Ever?* As in the second part of *forever?* I mean, I still had the tags on my eighteenth birthday presents. He said *ever.*

It seems crazy, but I was all in, maybe so far in that I wasn't sure how I was going to extract myself well enough to dig in to college. I'd be *that girl,* the one with the out-of-town boyfriend who skipped all the parties and scheduled her week around escaping for the weekend. I'd end up thirty years old with six kids, big hips, and bad style, wondering where all my potential went.

Maybe not. But it does happen.

July and August had been that magic space of time that you can only carve out during a summer vacation, like a break between two realities where all you have to do is be together. Weeks go by in a blur of sandy kisses, long swims, and reluctant good-nights. There's never enough time, and that Labor Day deadline makes everything so much more intense. I wondered if we'd ever be able to get back there in another setting, or if it would be impossible to replicate, like the way your hair looks when it dries in the sun.

In Massachusetts, everything seemed different. The architecture was different; the faces were different; the light was different. Even the bumper stickers were different. The future was long, and the possibilities for distraction were endless. I had no idea how big the world was or how much more trouble I could get myself into, but I definitely had a feeling this long-distance thing wasn't going to be easy.

LET YOUR GEEK FLAG FLY

TIKI LEFT FOR THE NIGHT AT around eight. I wondered if she was the one who'd end up being *that girl* and miss out on everything because of her boyfriend. She and Howard were going to hang out in his room and watch a movie. Twelve percent of me thought that was the lamest thing ever; the remaining 88 percent was totally jealous.

My plan was to stay in my room with the door locked. Tiki was the only person I'd talked to, and I wasn't sure I was up for repeating the whole "Hi, I'm Digit. The reason I have this crazy name is because I'm crazy. How 'bout you?" routine. But at around eight thirty there was loud music in the hallway outside my door. And then lots of voices and friendly shouting. I tried to think of what to do, pacing back and forth (this was barely one step in either direction). Was I going to swing open my door and find myself in the middle of a big party? There would be no sizing it up before I was fully involved. I looked through the peephole and saw complete darkness broken by a rhythmically flashing white light.

The banging on my door jolted me back to reality. It was urgent, emergency banging, and I had no choice but to open up. Standing there was a boy, six feet five, with a crew cut and a huge smile. "Wassup!!!!!" He dragged me by the hand into the hallway and started dancing with me, spinning me around in such a way that hid the fact that I was way too nervous to actually dance. Someone had covered the fluorescent hall lights in black paper and had placed a strobe light along the wall, making us all seem like we were moving in slow motion. I wondered who was behind this. Did someone actually have the foresight to bring a strobe light to college? Was it this big wild extrovert in front of me, who seemed intent on dragging everyone out of their rooms-slash-shells?

I have to admit that halfway through the first song I was having fun. It was too loud to talk, so I was spared the "You're name's what?" conversation. And the many, many flaws in my dancing style were masked by the lights flashing on and off. All anyone saw of me was a series of freeze frames. I was a flip book. It is impossible to tell that someone has no rhythm in a flip book. Someone handed me a warm beer and I nodded thank you, still dancing and spilling half on the floor.

There was a couple making out against my door, and I had the hardest time not staring at them. I mean, we just got here. How do people figure that stuff out so fast and so publicly? Meanwhile, the big guy was getting a little friendlier all the time. First just spinning me around by the hand, then putting his other hand around my waist, then breathing the breath of a beer-chugging dragon into my face. I had to move on. "Spin me," I mouthed, with the enthusiasm of a dance-show contestant. As soon as he spun me out, I let go of his hand to gracefully sashay over to the next group.

Okay, by "gracefully sashay," I mean I completely slid across the floor and into the partially open door of another dorm room. (Note to self: *When dancing on floors that are covered in spilled beer, opt for a rubber-soled shoe.*) I saw the big guy laughing at a distance and then become quickly distracted by another strobe light–protected dancing girl.

I was on the floor, a little sticky but safe. Two girls and a guy were behind me in the cramped room and somehow didn't notice my entrance. They were huddled together, silent except for a faint buzzing sound. After a few seconds there was a crash, followed by their enthusiastic cheers. I got up and completely dusted myself off before they noticed me.

"Who are you?" A heavily pierced girl in a camouflage T-shirt, plaid pajama bottoms, and combat boots made a face like maybe I hadn't showered.

"I'm Digit. I sort of fell into your door and—"

"Digit?" *Here we go.*

"Yeah, I'm good at math. What's your name?" I extended my hand to end the questioning.

The pierced girl said, "I'm Clarke. I mean, my name's Isabella Clarke, but I'm not exactly an Isabella, am I?" I looked her over and had to agree. An Isabella wouldn't have chosen the color Grim Reaper for her hair.

The other girl stepped in. "Hi. I'm Manuella." She was a Brazilian girl with long brown hair and severe black-rimmed glasses. "It's hard to say, so people call me Ella."

The guy said, "My name's Scott. Because that's what my parents named me. What's wrong with you people? Does everybody's name have to come with a book report?" Scott's clothing would have worked as a Steve Jobs Halloween costume: black mock turtleneck, blue jeans, wire-rimmed glasses.

They made no effort to ingratiate themselves to me any further. They stood shoulder to shoulder, forming a wall against the rest of the room. I wondered what to do. Clarke nodded at the door, as if to give me a suggestion. Scott reached toward the desk for a small remote control and quickly hid it in his pocket. In doing so, he must have accidentally pressed something. A small stuffed penguin marched out from under the bed, and with a frenzied press of a button it stopped.

Clarke let her hands fall at her sides. "You totally did that on purpose."

Scott was offended. "I did not."

"It's a joke how you can't keep a secret for five minutes. Fine. Show her." Ella stepped aside and revealed a pile of six fallen beer cans.

The vibe around me felt almost anticipatory, like I was supposed to have some big reaction. All I could think of was, "So you each had two beers?"

"Wow, she *is* good at math." Clarke rolled her eyes.

"No, look." Scott pressed a few more buttons, and two long arms grew out of the penguin's sides. To my true amazement, it proceeded to stack the beer cans into a pyramid. A green light flashed on its head, it backed up, and then shot a dart from its chest to knock the cans down. Again with the cheering.

"That's amazing. Where did you get it?"

Scott picked it up off the ground like it was a Chihuahua in a pink outfit. "I built her."

I was pretty impressed. I didn't know anything about engineering and couldn't even conceive of where you'd get started on a project like that. Like where would you even buy an On/Off switch? And how would you decide what kind of batteries to use? And what was it about this little penguin that made Scott call it a "her"? I decided not to ask any of these questions. I had a feeling I was in on some weird secret, but how could these three already have a secret?

So instead, this stuff came out, God help me. "I don't know anybody here besides Tiki. How come you guys seem to know each other so well? I mean, did you meet this morning and happen to find each other? Does that happen to everyone? Or am I just an outsider because I'm from California?"

They responded, rapid-fire:

Clarke: California?
Me: Yep.
Scott: You surf?
Me: No.
Ella: Obsessed with your car?
Me: No, but I collect bumper stickers.
Ella: Fine. Yoga?
Me: No.
Scott: Who's Tiki? Another long-story name?
Me: My roommate. I assume so.
Clarke: Fake boobs?

Me: Me? No. Probably not Tiki either.

Clarke: His glasses are fake and so are Ella's. Do you find that as hilarious as I do?

Me: Yes.

Lots of glancing at one another and then, "Okay."

Clarke sat down on one of the beds, and the other two sat on the bed across from her. I didn't know where to put myself so I flopped onto the floor, crisscross applesauce, like when I was five. Talk about feeling looked down on.

Clarke got up to shut the door. "So we met in a hackers' chatroom about six months ago and realized we were all going to be freshmen at MIT. Scott showed Ella and me the prototype for Clementine here, and we bonded over the sheer genius of it. There's a robotics competition in December, and no freshman team has ever won. I guess mainly because they haven't been working together for long enough. But we have." Nods, knowing glances.

"You really can't tell anyone," said Ella.

"What? That you guys had met before? Is that against the rules?"

Scott tented his fingers under his chin in such a Steve Jobs way that I sort of thought he was making a joke. "Not that. But we did mess a bit with the school's residential living system. Just to make sure that we'd all be in the same dorm."

"Actually, Ella and I are roommates, and we gave Scott the single across the hall. Lucky."

"So you're hackers." I was just trying to make sense of it, to straighten it out in my head. Was it harmless what they were doing? Were they criminals? Was it just super fun and a way to get the dorm-mates you wanted?

Those were not the questions I should have been asking myself. But if I'd known what questions to be asking I probably wouldn't have needed to ask them.

✦　–　✦

I hung out with those guys for a long time. I collected so much data on who they were and how hackers operate that I couldn't wait to be alone to process it all. They showed me some basic hacking techniques, just hacking into their own stuff. They were all so goodhearted, even Clarke with her sort of rough exterior. She whispered to me when I left, "You can hang with us, but do me a favor. No fake glasses." I laughed thinking of how long I tried not to seem like a nerd when neo-nerd was a carefully cultivated look around here.

I got back to my room by pretending to boogie down the hall. I waved my arms in the air, *woot-woot,* high-fived a few drunk people, and shoved that same kissing couple two inches to the left so I could reach my doorknob. I locked it behind me and threw myself on my bed. The first night of college had been a bit like drinking water from a fire hose. Overwhelming, but still refreshing.

I turned out the lights, and the moon cast the sinister pattern of the old leaded windows on the wall over my bed. Each pane had four rows of three rectangles, which minded their own business while a branch poked at them at irregular intervals. *Stop poking me,* I thought, and immediately missed my brother, Danny. He was three days away from starting his senior year and would surely sail through it with his patented mixture of fun, sweetness, and getting away with murder.

Murder . . . which brought me to the kidnapped man's 3-D artwork that threatened to pounce on me from across the room. With the music still booming on the other side of the wall, I decided to call John in L.A.

"Hey. How was the first night?"

"Interesting."

"How?"

"I danced. I met a bunch of hackers. They swore me to secrecy over some robot they built. And then I danced home. It was actually kind of cool." I felt better just talking to him.

"That sounds pretty good. I miss you."

"Maybe I should come home. I could be in Malibu in eight hours, and we could go to the beach." I heard a sigh.

"Don't tempt me. I thought about flying out there today and being that creepy boyfriend who shows up all the time. I don't even know what to do with myself without you here. I was thinking earlier of stopping by to see Danny, but that just seemed pathetic."

"Seriously, classes don't start for two days. I feel oriented already. Maybe I should come see you."

"I'll be in New York next week. And I'll be up to see you in two weeks. It'll seem like nothing someday." *Grownups.*

THINK OR PERISH

I WOKE UP AT TWO A.M., POSITIVE that someone was standing over my bed. The moon was still projecting a shadow on my wall, but no one was there. I kind of had to pee and weighed the creepiness of my room against the potential creepiness and stickiness of the dark hallway that led to the huge communal girls' bathroom. I decided I was being ridiculous and that I wasn't going to be able to hold it for four years, so I got out of bed and found my slippers. And my brand-new I'm-going-to-college bathrobe. All I needed was a big set of curlers to look exactly like my great-grandma Dorothy.

I poked my head out of my room and looked both ways down the dark hallway. The smell of stale beer was intense. I looked left and right maybe six times—I'd crossed highways with less caution. *It's a hallway, Digit.* I tiptoed into the darkness and moved toward the third door on the left, focusing on the reassuring light coming from under it. My heart was racing from I-don't-know-what as I finally pushed the door all the way open to flood the hall with light.

A guy was standing at the sink, in a towel, shaving. It took me a few beats to register: *A guy is standing at the sink, in a towel, shaving.* He turned to look at me. His sandy hair was wet and shaggy like he'd given it a once-over with the towel that was now wrapped around his waist, too low. Really, impossibly low. *How do men keep towels up when they have no* hips? Is there a special way to fasten it at the front? Maybe there's Velcro . . . I'd feel so much better if I knew there was a little piece of Velcro holding that tiny little flap . . . because it could definitely slip any second now, and he'd just be standing there . . .

"Hello?" He was saying something. And I was staring. I started shifting in my slippers from side to side. How long had I been staring at that most precarious spot where the top of his towel met the very, very bottom of his stomach? As my eyes lowered, I started to focus, as only I can, on the striped pattern of his towel. Every brand in America makes a striped towel, but this one had a break in the stripes so that every fifteen inches, the stripes stopped matching up. No, not every fifteen inches. Every fifteen, then six . . . I needed him to turn around to see the back. I couldn't break myself away from trying to force those stripes to meet. "Is there something the matter with you?" the guy said. *Uh, what was your first clue?*

"You're going to have to take off that towel." Oh my God. "No! Don't take off that towel!" I closed my eyes and tried to picture a perfect circle. I knew I looked completely nuts, but if I was going to recover, I needed to snap out of it and try to explain. But I didn't want to keep having to explain this, and certainly not to a mostly naked guy. "You know what's weird?" I opened my eyes. "I think I was sleepwalking. Just woke up! Wow! Now I'm awake. And maybe in the men's room? Hmm. I'll just . . ." I started backing up, not sure why I wasn't turning around to just get out of there. Maybe I was waiting for some acknowledgment that this happens all the time, that I was the third girl to walk in on him tonight. *Why is he walking toward me?*

"I'm Bass." He reached out a hand to me and, thankfully, secured his towel with the other. "I'm the RA on this floor. We'll be meeting in the morning. Fully dressed." Is it possible to have a little twinkle in your eye while standing half-naked and half-shaving-creamed in front of a total stranger? Unfathomable.

"Okay." I turned to go, managing to secure my eyes on the dirty floor where they should have been all along.

"The girls' bathroom is across the hall. It says 'girls' on the door." *Gee, thanks.*

I managed to get through the get-to-know-your-friendly-RA meeting without making any direct eye contact. I mean, isn't it some sort of sexual assault seeing someone in a towel? Yeah, I walked in on him, but still. Now that he was fully dressed in jeans and a T-shirt that said NEVER DO ANYTHING YOU WOULDN'T WANT TO EXPLAIN TO THE PARAMEDICS, I could actually look at him. He had an unnerving way of smiling with his eyes while barely lifting the corners of his mouth. His eyes were blue and lit up with amusement at almost everything, and I found myself staring at his mouth to see if it would curl up enough to match them. When he laughed his mouth was forced all the way into action, but when he smiled it was mostly his eyes. Sometimes I wish I could just gloss over the details.

A one-eared dog sat at his feet while he talked to us. "About your little party last night. This may come as a shocker, but there is no alcohol allowed in the dorms. If you thought maybe you were getting away with something, well, you were. I let that happen for a couple of reasons, and don't expect a repeat. First of all, it was the first night, and I wanted you all to let loose and maybe get acquainted. I can see you accomplished that." Laughter all around. The couple who had been making out against my door got a lot of looks. "And, second, because now you guys owe me. I am not allowed to keep a dog in here. And I don't know how I'd be able to do it without you guys knowing. It's only for a couple of weeks. His name's Buddy, and he's a rescue dog. I'll find him a home pretty soon, but you guys have to keep it to yourselves. Okay?"

I personally couldn't have cared less if he had a dog in his room. What was cool was that we all suddenly had the sense of community that comes with a shared secret. Bass waited until all twelve of us had nodded in agreement.

"You should also know that he can sniff out any illicit substances you might be keeping in your room, so as my first official act as your residential adviser, I advise you to get rid of it." We all looked at each other, trying to scope out any potential potheads. Bass got up and started to leave the room. "Now you have twenty minutes to clean up that hallway before the janitors show up and we're all busted. Mops and garbage bags are in the closet by the girls' bathroom." Putting his hand on my shoulder, he said, "This young lady should be able to show you where that is."

I'm not a huge blusher, and I'm not even that fair-skinned. But some kind of fiery redness shot out of my cheeks, and I had to completely bow my head to conceal it. Clarke's natural tendency to be personally offended by absolutely everything saved me. "Uh, yeah, Bass, we're all pretty smart. We can find the girls' bathroom."

After twenty minutes of mopping, bagging, and stashing, I felt comfortable with all the kids on my hall. Even the big guy who I was sure was going to grope me last night seemed fun and harmless. His name was Kevin, and he was from Topeka. He would forever be known as Kevin from Kansas. That seemed to be the tricky part of the first few days, just avoiding a bad nickname. I was glad to have brought my own.

I walked to the big freshman orientation breakfast with my new hacker pals and Tiki. Scott gave me a shove as we walked. "Um, sure you got a good-enough look at that RA, Digit?"

Tiki laughed. "Yeah, there's a little drool right . . . there, in the corner of your mouth. You may want to wipe that before your 'boyfriend' (*please don't get me started on air quotes*) visits."

Everyone laughed in a good-natured, it's-no-biggie sort of way. This alarmed me for two reasons: Was I really staring at him for so long that people noticed? Why were they acting like it didn't matter if I did? I mean, didn't girls in love not notice other guys?

The orientation breakfast was pretty fun. I stayed with the kids from my hall mostly but met some new people too. No one really knew anybody, so even the introverts were forced to introduce themselves. The dean gave a speech about new beginnings, and we ate scrambled eggs and bacon from chafing dishes.

When we got back to the dorm, it was surrounded by police cars. At first I thought something had happened to someone and was waiting for a stretcher to come out the front door. But the dorm would have been completely empty with all of the freshmen away at breakfast. We stood outside the yellow police tape and speculated about what might be going on.

"Somebody's taken Clementine!"

"Nobody's taken Clementine. No one even knows about Clementine." Ella was trying to sound reassuring.

"Who's Clementine?" Tiki asked.

"Except for Digit and now her, starting now," said Clarke.

Scott took this as permission to tell Tiki all about Clementine and the robotics competition that they were going to enter. It's funny how there are certain secrets that people don't mind sharing with everyone who will listen, as long as they preface them with "This is top-secret . . ."

Bass walked out with two cops. "Okay, I'll get them. But really, there's no reason to say anything about the dog in your report, right?" He told us that six rooms on our hall had been broken into in the past hour. "The police think it was a professional job, someone who knew what they were looking for and when you would all be away. Nothing seems to be missing though, so will you guys go up to your rooms and see if you notice anything?"

Scott raced into the building to make sure that Clementine was all right (she was). I walked in with Bass, unworried because I have nothing to steal but my laptop and a gold necklace that my grandmother gave me. "You didn't have to go to that breakfast. Were you here?"

Bass turned to me, and I saw the cut over his eye for the first time. "Yep. Lucky me. Mine was the last door they opened, and I was able to stop it with my head. Buddy went nuts and they ran off."

"What did they look like?"

"I gave a full description to the cops. What, are you, like, in law enforcement or something?" Eyes smiling, mouth barely. I hoped I would soon get used to this because I found myself spending an inordinate amount of time staring at his mouth, just checking for motion.

"Watch a lot of cop shows. Plus I'm curious about what kind of creepy guys were going through my stuff."

When we got to my room, I found that nothing was missing. They hadn't even taken my laptop. Bass ran his finger over the 3-D overlay in Adam Ranks's poster, which I was quickly learning was impossible not to do. He opened my closet and found only my winter coat hanging. "You sure nothing's missing here?"

"Nope. That's all I've got." I wasn't going to explain to him that my wardrobe consisted entirely of wash-and-wear foldables in three colors. He'd figure that out in time.

He nodded like that meant something. "Good for you."

I could have obsessed over the break-in. I could have dwelled on my safety. But classes started the next day: Principles of Chemical Science, Multivariable Calculus, Physics II, Communications, and Artificial Intelligence. My first class was Multivariable Calculus, and I arrived twenty minutes early and nabbed a center seat in the third row. The vibe in the big lecture hall was unlike any class I'd ever been in. The kids didn't look much different from the kids in my high school, except maybe they were more conservatively dressed. It wasn't until the class was over that I figured out what the difference was: Every single student wanted to be there. I mean, every one of them had busted their butts to get into MIT, and, just like me, they felt like this class was a reward for their hard work. People asked questions about things I'd never heard of, and it occurred to me that there was more for me to learn than I had even hoped. I could actually feel my cells accelerating throughout my body, like I was super alive instead of just regular alive. We were being fed by that lecture, the way some people feel at a museum or a concert or a sample sale. I looked around the lecture hall and thought: *These are my people.*

I met Ella for coffee after my first Artificial Intelligence class and asked her so many questions about computer science that she finally had to stop me. "Can we just take a break and talk about your old man boyfriend?"

"There's not that much to say." *There is so much to say!* "He's a really great guy, and he's coming to visit next weekend."

The thought of seeing John made my stomach flip. Every inch of me was aching to see him, to smell his neck, and to hold his hand while I walked.

"Is that going to be weird?"

"Why would it be?"

"I don't know, just having him here, staying at the dorm when he's like a 'real guy' with a 'real job.'"

"Don't do that."

"What?"

"The air quotes. It drives me crazy. It's like a conversation crutch where you want to use a word or a phrase but think it might be dopey so you put quotes around it to make it seem like those are someone else's words so you're not blamed for using them. He is a real guy with a real job. See what I mean?"

Ella laughed and proceeded to finish our entire conversation entirely in air quotes. "Okay, fine. I'm sure your 'boyfriend' will 'blend in' perfectly with the 'scene' here."

ROCK IS DEAD: LONG LIVE
PAPER AND SCISSORS

WHEN JOHN BUZZED UP TO MY dorm after those endless two weeks, I was suddenly shy to see him. What if we had nothing to talk about? What if the attraction was gone because my tan had faded? I stomped around my room, hoping that the sound of my boots would calm me. When I opened the door and saw him standing there in khakis, a gray cashmere sweater, and the slightest five o'clock shadow, I got so nervous that I couldn't stop talking. "Hey, come in. I mean, you can't stand out there, right? Let me get the door. Is that your bag? I've never seen you with luggage. How was the train?"

"Digit? Seriously? It's me." He pulled me into his arms and kissed me. I closed my eyes, and we were back in California and everything made sense. And just like I remembered, the kiss made me a little dizzy.

"Right, sorry. I freaked out for a second. I'm okay now." I rested my head on his chest and tried to gather my thoughts and steady my breath. It was so weird. I'd wanted him here so badly, but now that he was here, he just seemed so out of place. It's like when you're a little kid and you see your teacher at the supermarket. She's the same person, but out of context you're like: *Why don't you have chalk in your hand?*

"Hey, I'm nervous too."

What was it about his also being nervous that made this so

much better? I started to relax and kissed him again. "Okay, let's just be nervous, then. Want a tour?"

He laughed as he let me go and started to look around my room. "Hang on, where is all the crazy? No bumper stickers?"

I missed them too. There was no way to replicate the way I'd covered the walls of my room at home. Plus I promised my mom I'd make a little effort at dorm-room chic.

"It'd take me all year to cover these walls, and I'm trying to ease Tiki into the wackier side of Digit."

He walked over to where Adam Ranks's evergreen hung over Tiki's bed. "He's still missing, right? The story's kind of dying in the news—have you noticed that?"

Huh. "I haven't read anything about him since I've been here. It's like I forgot about the newspaper. This place is its own little world. Weird."

"We'll have to air you out a little. There's an Italian restaurant in Boston I want to try. I have a cab waiting. And then we can do some college stuff." He unzipped his bag and pretended to rifle around in it. "I know I put my toga in here somewhere . . ."

"Very funny. Let's go."

The first person we saw as we stepped into the hallway was Bass, wearing a black T-shirt that said I HAVE REASON TO BELIEVE RACCOONS ARE MOCKING ME and carrying a guitar case. "Hey, Digit."

I froze. "Hey. We were . . . um, this is . . ."

John reached out a hand. "I'm John."

"Bass. I'm the RA." Suddenly everyone was relaxed but me.

"Yeah, he's the RA." I was trying to regain my composure. I mean, was I the first girl to ever walk out of a dorm room with a guy? I felt like *I* was standing there in a towel. "John's my friend."

They both looked at me like I'd said something as dumb as, well, what I'd just said. John said, "Yep, I'm off to get my buddy here some dinner."

"Okay, you two have fun." Amused eyes, little smile. "But come by the coffeehouse later—my band's playing at ten. Tiki and your Three Stooges said they were coming."

When he was out of earshot, I gave John a serious shove. "Stop making fun of me."

"It's just too easy." He took my hand. "It's okay to have a boyfriend. You're all grown-up." I felt twelve.

"I know. I just . . . I didn't know if it was okay that you were staying here. And I didn't want him to think we were . . . I mean, we are. But I . . ."

John was beyond amused.

About four minutes into the cab ride, everything felt normal again. We were laughing about the unidentifiable smell in my dorm, and John said he couldn't wait to see the bathrooms. I started to tell him the story about meeting Bass half-naked but thought better of it. It's not even really a story, just an embarrassing moment that I probably wouldn't want to hear about if things were reversed.

At dinner he filled me in on everything at the FBI Terror Task Force. All the trainees were working long hours. He and his new friends Spencer and George were pretty much expected to be at the senior agents' beck and call around the clock. The three of them had joined a gym and regularly snuck out of the office to work out during dead time. He ran through a long list of places he wanted to take me for spring break, if we could ever make it cool with my parents. There was a village near Nepal he wanted me to see and a hotel outside the Brazilian rain forest that was actually built in a tree. We shared a salad and pasta and osso buco (must remember to look up what animal that is). Delicious.

John showed me photos of his new West Village apartment on his phone. It had a beautiful balcony and a view of the pastry shop across the street. There were a few pictures of the inside, but they were mostly of the old sycamore trees that line the street, taken from the balcony. One was of a sycamore tree perfectly centered between the pastry shop's two window boxes, orange pansies evenly distributed. These photos were edited just for me, and it occurred to me that there is nothing nicer than when someone has taken the time to know you.

"Send me that one, for my phone. It's perfect."

"Sure. It's probably good to have backup in case your reliable oak tree photo doesn't work. How is all that since you've been here?"

At first I thought he was teasing me. I mean, it's not hard to mock a girl whose brain has an unreliable Off switch. But the look on his face was more serious, and I could tell he really wanted to know. Believe me when I tell you, there are not a lot of people I'd have this conversation with. Maybe three.

"It's okay. I was a little overwhelmed when I first got here, so I felt a little on edge. A couple of times I thought I was going to slip into the overcomputing place. There was this towel with an irregular stripe, and Tiki tried to hang this poster that was . . . I don't even want to talk about it. But since classes have started, I feel like my brain has so much data to process that it kind of naturally shuts off when I'm done. I haven't had to pull out the oak tree photo to quiet my mind since I've been here. It's kind of like when Danny was little and we had to let him run around for an hour before dinner so he could sit still and eat. I wonder if there's really nothing wrong with me, but that my brain just needed more exercise."

"There's nothing at all wrong with you."

"Thanks." I fiddled with my napkin, completely nervous again. When I looked back up, John was staring at me.

"I'm glad you're here. I'm glad there's a place like this for you. Even if I miss you all the time. It's just right that you're here. You need it."

"Yep, the hamster needs her wheel." I'm embarrassed to report that he kissed me right there in the restaurant and that we sat so close to each other in the booth that we could have fit eight other people around us. It was a perfectly romantic date for two perfectly normal people. That was all I wanted.

The pit in my stomach returned as soon as the cab brought us back to campus. "So, really? Are you really ready to do this?"

"C'mon, Digit, I want to meet Tiki and the hackers and see you in your new natural habitat." He was totally relaxed and thought this was hysterical.

"Fine. Bass's band is playing at the coffeehouse; Tiki and those guys are definitely there. We'll go for an hour." I moved like I was taking the recycling out, in a hurry to get a necessary but annoying task out of the way. "C'mon."

When we walked into the coffeehouse, the band was so loud that I immediately stopped worrying that my friends and John would have nothing to talk about. They were a cover band with two guys on guitar, a keyboardist, and a drummer. Seeing Bass like that, totally in his element, I couldn't remember what he was like without a guitar in his hands.

Clarke, Ella, and Scott were crowded around a small cocktail table by the stage, alternately arguing about something and bobbing their heads to the music. The whole scene was like a silent movie, with arms waving and mouths moving but no words at all. Just really loud background music.

Tiki and Howard were at the bar. John and Tiki exchanged waves and *hello*s. John and Howard shook hands. John had his arm around me and seemed to be taking it all in like an anthropologist. I was just starting to relax when the band quit for a break. Silence.

"So, hey, you're the older spy guy I keep getting compared to." That was typical Howard, a little humorous and a little hostile.

"Yes. That's me. How are you measuring up?"

"Pretty good, not bad." Howard gave Tiki a little smirk. Ick.

Tiki likes to cut to the chase. "So is it weird to be back at college? Is this what Princeton was like? I mean, you should still be at college—you're only twenty-one, right? Do you feel like you missed out by finishing school so fast?"

"I don't even know what I missed out on. That's why I'm going to make Digit take me to every party on campus." He squeezed my hand.

"Oh my God, Digit. I love him." She wasn't even trying to direct this just at me. "He's handsome and sweet and in law enforcement. Hot!"

Howard was fidgety, like his skin was one size too small. "Wish your hero had been around two weeks ago for the big break-in."

John was looking directly at me when that comment registered. His face fell. "What break-in? Where?"

"Oh, has your girl been keeping things from you? It was big news during the first week of school." *Shut up, Howard*.

"What was? What happened?"

I started pinning my hair behind my ears, as if the mere fact of getting it to stay there was going to make this lie of omission okay. "Yeah. Didn't I tell you about that? There was a break-in at one of the dorms during the day. Campus security was called and the guys sped off."

"Which dorm?" He was talking only to me now.

Howard must have sensed I was in trouble and was going to keep twisting the knife.

"*One* of the dorms, Digit? It was *their* dorm, *their* hall. No one knew what he wanted—it's not like people keep lots of valuables around here. But he broke the lock to their room and took nothing, not even their laptops."

"Did you get a description? Why didn't you tell me? Where were you?"

"No. Because I knew you'd freak out. At an orientation breakfast."

John just shook his head. I couldn't tell if he was scared or pissed or both. He leaned in toward me and I was hoping for a kiss, but I got "We have to leave now." It was the exact same robot voice he'd used when he was about to save my life by throwing me out of a cab.

"Sure. Okay. Guys, we're gonna go. We'll just . . . we'll see you tomorrow."

We walked in silence back to my dorm. John was holding my hand but not like a boyfriend holds your hand, more like how your mom holds your hand to keep you from running out into traffic.

When we got to my room, he closed the door and locked it. He checked the locks on my windows. "What else haven't you told me?" His eyes were more hurt than angry.

I sat down on my bed and took a deep breath. "I didn't think it was important?"

"You didn't? Six months ago a huge terror organization was trying to kill you. And almost did. And you don't think it's worth mentioning a breaking-and-entering incident at your dorm? In your room?"

"I didn't want to upset you."

"Upset me? What about when they got you? Was I going to be upset then? What was I going to do then, Digit?"

He sat down next to me and put his head in his hands. He kept talking without looking at me. "This isn't a game. You were in real danger; we both were. And sure, I was falling for you, but more than that I was just doing my job, relying on my training. That's the only reason we survived. And now when I think about you, with a gun to your head, I just freeze. I'm so far away now, and I'm getting so paranoid that even if I were here, I don't know if I'd be clearheaded enough to protect you again."

I tried to think of something to say to make him feel safer. Which is funny because I was the one theoretically in danger. I had nothing.

He got really quiet and lay down on my extra-long, extra-narrow dorm bed.

"Um, can I . . . ?"

John scooted over and opened his arms to me. I lay down and had to shift around a bit to fit against him. His heart was beating faster than usual, and his jaw felt tense against the top of my head. Feeling his stress, I realized how much I'd been in denial about everything that had happened. And, ahem, this wasn't exactly how I'd imagined our romantic reunion night.

"I'm sorry. I just try not to think about all that stuff. It's just easier to move on." I turned onto my stomach so he'd have to look at me. "And, yeah, I was kind of freaked out about the break-in, but I guess I didn't want to go there. You know it's kind of like a pimple. If you keep messing with it and focusing on it and glopping all that goop on it, it seems to last forever and take over your life. But if you ignore it, it usually goes away on its own."

John let out an annoyed breath.

"What?"

"Nothing. Well, that's just a little childish. Ignoring your problems doesn't make them go away." *Oh, yes, he did.*

The word *childish* echoed in my ears. I'll admit now that maybe bringing up pimples in this situation wasn't the quickest path to getting the romance back on track. I'll have to check with *Cosmo* on that one. But *childish?* Really?

"I'm not ignoring a problem. The problem is solved. Jonas Furnis's guys are caught; they're gone. The pimple has resolved itself. Why am I going to keep thinking about it? I'm not going to keep buying Clearasil when it's been gone for three months!" I knew I had to get off the pimple thing, but when an analogy works it's hard to let go of it. And then I sat up to face him, hoping I'd seem more sane. "I just want to move on. I don't want to fight the bad guys or be on the run. I just want to be here, doing what I'm doing. And be with you, of course."

He brushed my hair from my face. "I feel like I can't leave. Like I should quit my job and be your bodyguard."

"Sounds good to me." There was an opening where I thought I could get away with kissing him. But he just shook his head.

"That's the problem—I feel like I could do that. I could move up here and build some sort of a force field around you so that you could stay safe and become who you need to become. But I've already quit one job to be with you. I'm scared I'm going to do it again." He put my hair behind my ear but stared at my shoulder. "You know how you're always worried about being *that girl*? Well, I'm *that guy*. It's insane."

"What if who I'm supposed to become is just your girlfriend?"

"Don't say that."

"Why?"

"It terrifies me. That's not who you are."

"How about I decide who I am?"

"I'm sorry, I know. I just feel like we're a little out of control." When he finally looked at me, he said, "Do you ever feel like we'd both be a lot better off if we just put this whole thing on hold?"

No. Never. Not even one time for one second. "Sometimes."

"I mean, think of all the things you are going to miss by having me here or you being in New York."

None, no things. I have just calculated a list of exactly zero-point-zero things that I am going to miss. "Sure, but we can figure it out, right? The balance. Like we talked about. When I'm here, I'll be here; and when I'm with you . . ."

I've had this dream a bunch of times where I'm driving a car and I'm trying to steer it straight, but it keeps turning into a tree or toward a cliff or something. I wake up feeling exactly like I felt in this moment. My voice was threatening to crack and my mind was racing, searching for the Rewind or at least the Pause button. We sat in the most gruesome silence. I stayed sitting, legs crossed to make a little barrier around me so that he wouldn't be able to feel how fast my heart was beating.

Finally, he sat up to face me, taking both of my hands in his. "There is no balance. When I am with you, I am completely off balance. It's all about you and us, and I completely lose track of myself. I don't know how I'm going to really start my career when my mind is so split. And you . . . this place is your dream come true, and you only get it for four years. To hear you saying maybe you just want to be my girlfriend . . . I can't let that happen to you." He wiped the tear that I'd been ignoring off of my cheek.

What's happening? Are you breaking up with me?

"It's not breaking up." Even my internal monologue was turning on me.

"An hour ago you loved me."

"And an hour from now I'll still love you. But we're going to give up too much of ourselves for this. Maybe when we're . . ."

"I think you should go."

"No, no. Let's talk about this. I don't want you to think I'm not . . ."

"I'm asking you to leave right now." The big tears—the ones that come with sobs and snot and puffy eyes—they were close. I needed him out of there. *Now.*

He picked up his bag, the one without the toga, and leaned over to kiss me on the forehead. "I don't think you understand how I . . ."

"Please go." As soon as the door closed behind him, the tears came in force.

TODAY IS THE TOMORROW YOU WORRIED ABOUT YESTERDAY

AT THE BEGINNING OF OCTOBER, I went to a lecture about how evaporative cooling is the primary mechanism responsible for the stabilizing effects observed for gas phase additives. Maybe not the most romantic topic in the world, but the idea of cooling and stabilizing made me think of John. I guess everything did. It seemed to me that the initial intensity of a relationship has its place, like the extra power a jet engine needs to get off the ground. If we could have hung on until we hit a cruising altitude, the cooling off would have been a welcome break. If cooled gases result in structural stability, maybe it would have been the same for us.

It had not been one of those long and messy breakups. The morning after he left, he called me at eight. I was sound asleep, having been up most of the night.

"Hey," he said.

"Hey."

"This wasn't how this weekend was supposed to go."

"Nope."

"I don't think you understand how much I love you."

"Here's what I understand." The cobwebs were clearing from my head, and my eyes stung from all the crying. "You love me so much that you can't be with me. It's not me; it's you. You need your space for your career. I've turned into a clingy freak. I get it. Here's what I need you to understand. You broke my heart. Again. And I'm going to get over it. But not if you keep calling me to see if I'm okay. You've made sure I'm not okay. Got it?"

"You sound really angry." *Thanks, Dr. Phil.*

"I am. Please don't call me back." And I hung up because I'm super tough. Well, I hung up feeling kind of tough because I'd been practicing that little speech all night. Then I just started crying again.

I'd done the self-indulgent breakup thing before. Same guy, same feeling. And the thought of wasting another six weeks crying, shoveling ice cream down my throat, and reciting the lines to *The Notebook* made me angrier than I already was. I was in my own personal heaven, with my whole life ahead of me, and I wasn't going to let John ruin it with his "We're too out of control" and "Maybe we need some time" garbage.

At least that was my mantra during daylight hours. At night it was harder. I let myself cry when I thought it would make me feel better. I'd replay that last scene in my head, sure it was the pimple talk that sealed my fate. And I'd type endless texts that I'd never send. Some frequent repeats were:

Was this whole thing a joke?
Can I come see you this weekend?
Do you ever think about me?
I love you
I hate you
Can we talk?

Honestly, I never sent them. Because I'm disciplined like that.

Other things that made me think of John: all music that had played on the radio that summer, steak, any variety of tree, the sound of a foreign language, men in suits. I was careful to shy away from all of these triggers, but some things were impossible to avoid. Even the back of my hand made me think of what the back of my hand used to look like when he held it. How are you supposed to avoid seeing your hands?

But I jumped into my classes and joined a mathematics methods club. It's called the Roaming Numerals because they travel around New England competing in math competitions. It's awesome. Clarke was trying to get me to join the Hackers Alliance, tempting me with access to the inaccessible and free pizza.

On the first weekend that I would have been in New York with John, I heard Professor Halsey speak for the first time. It was an overview of his research in nanotechnology, which promised to change everything about the way we fuel our homes, grow our food, and perform brain surgery. His work looks at changing things on a nano level, by altering matter that is a nanometer in size. He said this: "A nanometer is how long your fingernail grows in a second." I almost passed out. I mean, a piece of regular computer paper is 100,000 nanometers thick. How can you change something so small? And then how can the result of changing something on that level be so huge? I've heard people on TV describe the moment their lives changed—a near-death experience, a new baby, a great idea, love at first sight. I was surprised to find out that mine would be at an under-attended lecture by an eighty-year-old man in a chemistry lab basement. (And it was also not lost on me that I would have missed this if I'd gone to see John in New York.)

Halsey was not charismatic or even engaging, but his research was so brilliantly thought out and his findings so clearly groundbreaking that I felt like he was unlocking a vortex of information that would change science forever. I ran home and downloaded every single one of his published research papers and read until three a.m. They were pure poetry. I had a thousand questions and even more ideas. There was no doubt in my mind that his work was my future. I knew that I could help him with his research and fantasized that I could take it to the next level. Professor Halsey's destiny was tied to mine; I just had to meet him.

On Monday morning I marched over to his office to offer my services. Sitting behind a desk as gatekeeper to his office was Bass. *How many jobs does this guy have?* "Sorry, Digit, Professor Halsey doesn't employ freshmen. I started this gig last year as a sophomore and had to beg for it."

I wanted to say, *Yeah, but you're wearing a T-shirt that says* ON THE OTHER HAND, YOU HAVE DIFFERENT FINGERS, *and while I want to tell you that I have a bumper sticker that says that on my wall at home, and it honestly is one of my very favorites, I really should mention that I am a thousand times more qualified for this job than you are.* Instead I said, "I know I'm a freshman, but I'm . . . well, I have this . . ." I had to stop myself. I realized that at MIT I wasn't that different from anybody else. Ah, the irony! How long had I spent trying to wrap my head around my differentness? And now that I had, I wasn't so different at all. You couldn't throw a paper airplane without hitting a genius around here.

I tried a more direct approach. "I'd really like to talk to him for a second if he's free. I stayed up all night."

"He's not here, and he's never free. But I'll tell him you say hi."

Rewind and replay this scene every single day that week. I wrote letters and sent my resumé and high school transcripts. I gave him an essay expressing my thoughts on my favorite one of his research papers. No luck. On Friday Bass asked me to kindly stop calling. And loitering.

So, instead, I took a part-time job working for Ernest Marcello, a math professor who was trying to use mathematical algorithms to predict the economic impact of tripling the use of nuclear power, adjusted for the human health risks. I applied for the job and was hired to start immediately, and it took me two weeks to realize why no one else wanted it. The research was completely bogus, the professor was insane, and the entire project seemed intended to justify his presence on campus while he wrote a spy novel in his spare time. But it gave me access to a big chunk of the library of ongoing scientific research at MIT, so I stuck with it.

My parents and Danny flew in for parents' weekend in mid-October. Tiki's parents couldn't come because her great-grandmother was in the hospital, so she went down to Virginia instead. We had a family dinner in Cambridge that first night, and I'm pretty sure I never stopped talking. My dad was happier than I'd ever seen him, like some lifelong dream was finally materializing before his eyes. My mom fussed over my hair (roots!), my room, and the below-seventy-degrees weather.

My dad kept his arm around me for the whole walk back to the Marriott, forcing me to walk as slowly as he wanted me to. "You're okay?"

"I like to think so."

"I mean about the John thing. You're really over it? I was concerned that the breakup would ruin your freshman year."

The great thing about MIT was that no one really knew John, and no one ever asked about him. Over time I was able to sort of shut him out of my mind because there was so much else going on. But my dad's overall dadness cracked me a bit, and it felt good to start crying. We walked very slowly.

"It's fine. I mean obviously not fine. But he's right that maybe it was too intense, and that it's hard to be in college having a relationship with someone who's not. I just can't believe we'd go from being that close to not even talking at all. He's just totally dropped out of my life."

"But aren't you the one who told him not to contact you?"

"How do you know that?"

"Mr. Bennett called. He was very upset, wanted to know what his idiot son had done this time, to quote." See, my dad could totally do that, without relying on air quotes.

"He called me childish. But I was a little hard on him."

"I can imagine. Poor guy."

38

"Why do I feel like you're on his side?"

"I'm always on your side. You know that. It's just that I kind of feel like I owe him."

"What? For saving my life? Seriously? Are we going to keep giving him points for that? If I just send him a thank-you note, can we call it even?"

Dad laughed and tightened his grip around my shoulder. "Sure, it's nice that he saved your life. But I feel like I owe him for loving you in the right way." I didn't say anything because I was pretty sure I was going to start to cry again. "I always dreaded meeting your first boyfriend. I wondered who would ever be good enough for my daughter. And this summer I was sitting in the yard with John, and he started telling me how worried he was about ruining your time at MIT. He said he always wanted to be adding something to your life and was afraid he'd be taking something away from you in college. I didn't have an answer for him, but I thought to myself: *This must be what 'good enough for my daughter' looks like.*"

"Boy, is this not helping."

"I know. But I'm not sure it's fair for you to be acting like he ended it."

Sometimes I'm not so crazy about people being honest with me. "I miss him so much, Dad."

Dad squeezed my shoulder. "Life is long, sweetheart. You never know. In the meantime, you have all this freedom so that you can make the most of your time here."

"Isn't freedom just another word for nothing left to lose?" I was quoting one of his favorite old songs.

"Oh, you've got a lot left to lose, sweetheart."

Danny and I left my parents at the Marriott and went back to my dorm.

"How many people die from hypothermia here every year?" Danny was rubbing his hands together and banging on the radiator, a trick to spontaneously produce heat that he'd seen in a movie.

"I know, right? It's fifty degrees, and I feel like I'll never get warm again. January's going to be ugly."

Danny walked around my room, picking up everything in his path and examining it. "I still can't believe you're in college. And that you live so far away. I'm assuming you like it because you didn't shut up at dinner."

Could he possibly be trying to tell me he missed me? I hadn't really thought about him alone in the house with Mom and Dad, table for three every night. "I definitely miss you guys, but it's been pretty amazing being here. I mean, it's how I imagine coming out is for gay people: it's like I am finally allowed to talk about all this stuff that's been floating around in my head all these years. And there's so much stuff I don't know that I sometimes can't sleep just thinking about it."

Danny was smiling. "Nerd sanctuary. Awesome." He ran his finger over Tiki's Adam Ranks poster. "You keep a kidnapped guy's artwork just to remind you of the good old days?"

Uh, yeah, hello, other subject that keeps me up at night. "No, and I am thinking I may accidentally destroy that poster."

Danny was shaking his head but still staring at the poster. "Don't destroy it. This 3-D overlay thing he does — it looks like it's alive."

Danny and I decided to go for a walk around campus, figuring it was probably just as cold outside as it was in my room. I took him around the Brain and Cognitive Science building and past the Computer Science and Artificial Intelligence Lab. I showed him where Professor Halsey's office was. I told him about my dream job and how I knew that it was just a matter of time and patient stalking before it was mine.

"Digit, you are one nutty squirrel." He pulled off my hat and messed up my hair like he used to do when I was seven. Ahead of us, we saw a couple kissing on a bench, feverishly and without any regard for the dropping temperature. Danny whispered to me, "Get a room. And an electric blanket." I started to laugh, but then saw that it was Howard. And that blonde he was with was not, I repeat not, Tiki.

I didn't say anything to Danny, just shuffled him ahead and looped back around to my dorm. I took his arm to steady myself. My first reaction was rage. I felt as if my hair could have spontaneously turned red and stood straight up on its own. Then I felt sad, so sad and disappointed for Tiki, who was completely committed to their relationship and had gone to MIT just to be with him. And then panic. I couldn't tell her. There was no way that the words would come out of my mouth, no way. I was not going to be the messenger, the one to break her heart with an offhanded *Guess what I saw on my walk this weekend?* No way.

Looking back, which I'm really going to have to start doing a lot less of, telling Tiki the truth about Howard would have been a lot easier than the mess I got into for keeping my mouth shut. And by "mess," I mean stuff like assault, abduction, and felony treason. You know, a mess.

I BRAKE FOR HACKERS

I LOGGED EXACTLY NINETY MINUTES AT THE Copley Place mall with my mom, less than I'd promised but more than she expected. I got an army green midweight jacket, a brown sweater (my choice), and a gray sweater with navy blue cuffs (her choice). I swear sweaters are getting more complicated every year.

Tiki got back the next day right as my family was leaving for the airport. My mom threw her arms around her. "Darling, how is your great-grandmother?"

"She's a goner." Tiki looked around and laughed. "No, sorry, not dead. But she's gonna be. She's ninety-eight, and everything's starting to go, so I'm pretty sure she'll be done this week."

Danny gasped. "Done? Like a turkey?"

"Sorry, I know it sounds crass, but we've got a lot of people on this planet. She's been here almost ninety-nine years and has done a lot of great stuff. But I mean, let's keep this system moving, you know? Out with the old, in with the new." She started unpacking and talking about how much better the weather was in Virginia until my family left.

"Tiki, are you okay?"

"I am. I mean, honestly, I love my great-grandmother, but she can't go on like that with a machine breathing for her. I really hope she goes soon."

"I read that ventilators can keep a person alive as long as

their . . ." She wasn't listening to me at all. "Is there something else?"

She plopped down on her bed, crossing her impossibly long legs beneath her. "It's Howard. I'm probably just being stupid, but I feel like there's something going on with him. I can just feel it, you know?"

Yes, I know, feel it. Please. "What do you mean?"

"Well, like last night I called him six times and he never picked up. You know how that guy always has his phone at the ready. So this morning he said, 'Yeah, sorry, babe. I went to bed early.' He never goes to bed early. Ever."

This was hardly a smoking gun, but I was starting to feel more and more relieved. She went on: "And *then* I called him on my way back from the airport to see if he wanted me to stop by, and he said, 'No, sorry, babe. I'm turning in early.' What the hell, right?"

Anyone without the information that I so unfortunately had would have suggested that maybe he was sick. I decided to feed the beast. "That is weird. What do you think it means?"

"I don't know. I can't imagine he's . . . I mean, he wouldn't . . . Let's check Facebook." She pulled out her laptop and started banging away.

"Tiki, if he's doing something he doesn't want you to know about, he's not going to post about it." *Duh.*

"But someone else might have. I just need to see what was happening on campus last night. Someone's got to have a photo." It didn't take long for her to find a photo of Howard dancing with that blond girl at Simmons Hall.

"Oh," I offered, sympathetically.

"It's not enough." Tiki was up and pulling at her hair, adjusting the spikes like she was trying to secure a clearer connection to the universe. "I'm not going to go down as the crazy high school girlfriend who overreacted to a photo on freakin' Facebook. I need proof. I need an eyewitness."

Actual real-life eyewitness said, "But there is no eyewitness."

We went back and forth like this for a long time before Tiki decided we needed to hack into his Facebook account and read his private messages. "Let's try the obvi passwords. It used to be Tiki and my birthday. No? Okay, try Tiki is a ten, all one word. No? His dog's name is Snoopy?" We exhausted everything we could think of—including the name of the girl in the photo.

"You could just ask him."

"I can't. I don't want to get into a whole big thing and come out of it seeming crazy because he's just denying it. He has a way of turning everything around and making me seem like I'm paranoid. I'll end up apologizing to his cheating ass. This has happened before."

I kept trying logical passwords, then adding numbers to the end. It could take a century to crack a code this way, but I was getting hypnotized by it. Snoopy124, Snoopy125. Tiki may have read my mind. "Before you slip into the Digit Zone, why don't we download one of those brute force programs that go through every possible iteration to crack a password? It can run while we sleep."

Scott had showed me one of these programs on that first night in the dorm. They were pretty simple; they just tried various combinations of letters and numbers in an orderly way. Eventually the code would be cracked. They were written in any one of the coding languages I'd been learning in my computer science class: C, LISP, Perl, Java. They were really beautiful languages, some better than others, but they were all like paints that you could use to either create a big red circle or the *Mona Lisa*. The power was in the mind of the programmer. I'll admit it: The idea of just pressing Go to run one of these programs left me a little flat. It's like painting by numbers or making a cake from a box. What's the point?

"We could get into a lot of trouble if someone caught us buying one of those programs. How would we explain it? If you'd just give me a little while, I can write one. We'll run it, get the password, and I'll erase it. The perfect crime."

"You're going to write a program? Because I'm suspicious of my boyfriend?"

"No. Of course not." I could hear how stupid I sounded. "You should probably just talk to him." I got under my covers and felt a little relieved. I mean, I'm not a hacker, and there's no reason for me to learn to be one. Just so that I could prove that Tiki's boyfriend was a scumbag. Scumbag. Scumbag1, Scumbag2, Scumbag3. Okay, I had to write that program.

I opened my laptop in the dark and got to work. I didn't know exactly what I was doing, of course. I just wrote a little code, ran it, tinkered with it, and started again. And I was done at eight a.m. It wasn't what they'd call an elegant program, but I'd go back and fix that. Probably before lunch. But it ran, and within twenty minutes, we had his password: Luckydevil. Not for long.

About a week later, after Tiki had found a ton of flirty messages in Howard's inbox and dumped him without an apology, I was still writing code. I had my laptop with me everywhere, massaging my program to make it run faster and do more with fewer iterations. I never even intended to use it again, but it was creative and addictive and orderly. I really couldn't stop. Intervention, anyone?

I ran pieces of it by Ella and went to Clarke when I got really stuck. They were delighted that they'd brought me into the inner circle of hacking. To them, hacking was more of a lifestyle than a means to an end. Besides the dorm room switch-around, they never benefited from it. The hacking was just about proving they could get in, and then get out. I wanted to show them the whole program, but I wasn't quite ready to let it loose. Plus the truth is that as much as this was just an exercise for my mind, it was a hacking tool. And I had actually used it to hack. A little.

"You're going to have to give this up." Tiki caught me hunched over my desk at noon on a beautiful fall day. "I want you to delete it."

Delete it? Right. It was becoming stronger and better every day.

"I miss the days when you were heartbroken and mopey. I could really go there with you now. Could you give the hacking a rest?"

"No." I didn't look up.

"Listen, Thursday night there's a toga party."

I had to look up. "There are really toga parties?"

"Apparently. They're for real people, away from their laptops, who want to have a good time. Are you listening?" She swung my chair around so we were eye to eye. "Howard's going to be there with that girl. And I look really hot in a toga, trust me. You're going with me. And we're going to have normal college fun. Clear?"

"Yes."

"No matter what?"

"I promise."

"Now this is going to be epic." Truer words were never spoken.

I did as I was told and shut Oscar down before leaving for work on Thursday. (Oh, yeah, Oscar was my pet name for the program. Not that I was going to say it out loud, but when you get sort of attached to something, you develop a certain affection for it. The program was like a tenacious little pug, happily blasting his way through firewalls, wagging his little tail as he went. A perfect Oscar.) After work I'd meet Tiki back in the dorm to get all toga'd up. This was one of ten things that week that only John would have thought was funny. I composed a clever text and deleted it.

My promise was nearly derailed by Professor Marcello and his bogus nuclear research lab. He needed information for his Friday morning presentation to the committee that funds his research. (Again, by "research," I mean his spy novel.) It wasn't that much work—I just had to take a ton of data and present it in a way that was easier for them to understand. The problem was that it was going to take me forever to get the data. He usually let me know what data he needed a few days in advance, and I would have time to find it online or submit a request to the proper government authority. The government agencies generally approve your request for information within twenty minutes but won't actually give you the document until six to thirty-six hours later. It was my bad luck that the information I needed was from the U.S. Department of Defense. And that they take forever to deliver documents. Professor Marcello assured me that I'd have what I needed by eleven p.m. on Thursday and could complete my work then. Goodbye, toga party.

So what was I supposed to do? Really. I already had Oscar running at a pretty advanced level. I'd just have to try a few things to take it up about a hundred notches. I mean, I made a promise and sort of wanted to prove to myself that I could go out and be normal. Who knew, maybe I'd look hot in a toga too? It took a lot longer than I thought to get into the DOD, but by six p.m. Thursday night I had the document I needed. By eight p.m. I was done with my work and back in my room getting decked out in a white sheet. At worst, it was a victimless crime. At best, it was a timing difference.

SAY NO TO PEP

DRESSING FOR A TOGA PARTY IS pretty straightforward for anyone who's ever seen *Animal House* or has Internet access. The necessary materials are a white sheet and maybe a little ivy for your hair, for extra credit. How hard could this be? Very.

Tiki was, as promised, seriously hot in her toga and all ready to go by the time I got back to our room. She had a sheet and an ivy crown waiting for me, and I was completely focused on being a good sport. I'd been a drag for the past few weeks, flipping between my obsession with my ex-boyfriend and my obsession with Oscar. But now I was there and I was game. But not for an off-the-shoulder toga.

"But that's what a toga is. And you'll show a little shoulder . . ."

"Put me in something asymmetrical, and I'll be showing a little seizure."

"Fine." Tiki made me a two-shouldered toga that draped down the center in a way that I could deal with. But to compensate for the frumpy way my shoulders were covered, she took a pair of scissors to the bottom, turning my toga into a mini. "Nice. Let's go."

The second I walked into the party, I regretted going. I longed to be back at my desk in Marcello's office waiting for documents and tinkering with Oscar. A toga party, as it turns out, is just Halloween's Roman sister. And I can't stand Halloween. All the girls, and a lot of the guys too, took this as an opportunity to show as much skin as possible. I was sure I was the only person in the room wearing a bra. The energy in the room was kicked up about thirty notches from the energy at a normal party, and I blamed the sheets.

"Digit, you seem like a dud. And I need you to focus. I'm not going to tell you to have fun, but I am going to tell you to act and look like you're having fun. Howard just walked in right behind you." She threw her head back laughing, like she'd just heard her first knock-knock joke. "Now you. You laugh too." I started to laugh a little. "More. I'm funny. Get into it. I'm the life of the freakin' party." Tiki was definitely teetering on the brink of wacko. So I started laughing harder and then for real at the insanity of standing there in a mini-sheet pretending to be hilarious.

"What's so funny?" Bass was standing there with a girl. Said girl was wearing a seriously slutted-up toga, cut short and barely covering the one obligatory shoulder. Bass was in khakis and a plain white T-shirt. Plain.

"Where's your toga?" I felt so stupid. How could he get away with not wearing a toga? It seemed like cheating.

"I don't wear sheets. This is Tammy. Tammy, this is Digit and Tiki. They live on my hall."

"Hi!" Tammy seemed kind of drunk. Or annoying. Or too perky? Or not quite perky enough? I'm not sure what crime I was trying to pin on her, but I did not like Tammy.

"We're going to go dance." Tiki pulled me over to the other end of the room closer to the band. There were enough people dancing that I could kind of blend in and only partially embarrass myself. It's funny how in a big crowd no one really sees you at all. We were just one big mass of skin and flowy white cotton, and, well, after a few songs, I decided I kind of liked toga parties. At least it was different from the nightmare I imagined — the one where there's a big circle of people around me watching me try to bust a move. No one needs to see that. No one.

The band took a break, and we found Tammy and Bass by the keg. "So, Bass. No guitar tonight?" Tiki poured herself her second beer. I would not have normally mentioned it, except that she drank it like a marathoner on mile twenty-one and immediately poured herself another.

"No. I'm not playing tonight, just a spectator. Slow down there, Tiki. I don't want to have to report you." He was half kidding, but also half not.

I decided Tammy was actually too perky—that was the problem. She chirped, "Bass, you totally should play tonight! You know, that's where I met him! A few weeks ago at the coffeehouse, he was playing with his band! What a night! Unforgettable!" *Yep, I remember it well.* "There they are!"

Tonight's band came over, and they all gave Bass that half-handshake, half-hug thing that guys do. Introductions all around while Tiki poured herself another beer without Bass noticing.

"What's with you? Slow down," I mouthed. She nodded her head to the corner of the bar in response. And there was Howard with a third girl. Not blond and not Tiki. A really painfully pretty brunette. "He's a jerk."

"I know. And I'm going to go tell him."

"No." I grabbed her arm. "You're not." And that's when I realized that Tiki was on a path to making bad choices that were going to lead to really, really bad choices.

I turned to Bass for help, as he was in a position of semi-authority here, but he wasn't there. The music started up again, and all eyes went back to the stage. The band was gone, and it was just Bass onstage with an acoustic guitar playing the first few bars of "Crash Into Me." If you looked up "cheap tricks to get girls to swoon" in the dictionary, you would find an audio link to that song. And while I, too, can easily fall victim to such cheap tricks, I was amazed by the mass of girls that made its way closer to the stage, powerless drones. And no offense to Dave Matthews, but if you put that song in the hands of a younger, maybe handsomer guy who has the sense not to wear a toga to a toga party . . . well, it shouldn't be legal.

Tammy was front and center. I couldn't see her face, but I could imagine its perky delight. I pulled Tiki into the crowd, partially to see better and partially to widen the distance between Howard and her. She had filled her cup again and seemed a little wobbly.

"Tiki, just listen to the music. He's good, right?"

"Sure. But let me go back there. I just wanna tell him . . . I hate him so much."

"Who doesn't? Now stay here." I put my arm around Tiki to keep her stable and close and watched Bass like the rest of the groupies. What was it about a guy on a stage? What was it about a guy with a guitar? Why was he looking right at me? *He's looking right at me.* I went completely still and completely flushed. It's almost like if that person onstage looks directly at you, they are redirecting all the energy they're getting from the crowd toward you. It felt like a laser to the head. I had to look away.

And when I did, I noticed that Tiki was gone. She'd slipped out of my grip and was making her way toward Howard. I went after her. "Tiki. Stop. You are going to hate yourself tomorrow. Do not go talk to him. Let's dance a little. Then we'll go home."

"No! You can't stop me. I need to talk to him. I need to tell him how much I hate him . . . And how much I love him . . . and he has to take me back . . ." *Oh my god, this is worse than I thought.*

I dragged her, all five feet ten inches of her increasingly wobbly limbs, back toward the stage. I kept one arm around her waist and waved the other at Bass. I caught his eye, and he gave me a little upward nod as he sang. *No, I was not saying hi.* I ran through a mental list of universal gestures and only came up with the finger across the throat, meaning kill it or death. I combined that with a finger toward Tiki and a nod toward Howard and the brunette. Repeatedly. Until he finally understood and wrapped up the song a few verses early. My apologies to the disappointed girls, but Tiki was getting heavy and it is a pretty long song.

"Hey, thanks, guys," he said into the microphone over what should have been enough screams and applause to shake Tiki back into sobriety. No such luck. I held her up while he put down someone's guitar and jumped off the stage toward me.

"Is she okay?"

"God, I'm fine. Just let go of me. I need to talk to Howard."

"Got it. Let's get her out of here. But make it look normal. I don't want Howard to think she's a mess." So in the most dignified way that we knew how, Bass and I each put an arm around Tiki and escorted her past Howard into the night. As we passed the bar, Bass laughed, too loud. "You're right, this is kind of lame. Where's the other party?"

When we got outside, we let Tiki take a break on the grass for a bit. I had a bad feeling about her nice white sheet on that damp grass. And she no longer looked hot at all. We stood and watched as she cried, the streetlight making her look even more tragic than she was. "Okay, I'm fine now, just let me go back in. I'll be cool. I just want him to know how much I miss him . . ."

"No chance." Bass pulled her up and put his arm around her waist and started walking back to the dorm. He turned back to me. "A little help?"

We made it back to our room and deposited Tiki on her bed. Bass went to his room and got her a bottle of water and waited while she drank it. "Just let me go to sleep . . ." Tiki passed out as I struggled to move her under the covers.

"Our work here is done."

"Thank you. You going back out with Tammy?" The eternal question: *What is wrong with me?*

"No. I'm going back out with Buddy." He turned to leave and stopped. "Wanna come?"

"Can I change?" I suddenly felt like an idiot in my super-mini toga. These things really only work in a large group.

"I insist."

Back in my fashion comfort zone, I headed out into the night with Bass and Buddy. It was completely dark except for the streetlights. They were the old-fashioned kind, painted black, that let out a dull light. Exactly the right amount of light.

"Do you do this every night?"

"Save drunk girls from humiliating themselves? Most nights."

"The walking."

"I do. Buddy needs a lot of exercise or he tears up my room. Plus I like to be out here. I'm like a night watchman. During the day I check in on the trees. Somebody's got to do it."

"You have different trees out here. Like those old maples on Eastman Court. And the little cluster of weeping willows behind the Stata Center? Everything's different here than in L.A."

"I bet. For one, I hear people don't walk in L.A."

"We don't. We like our cars. And the leaves don't change. Which I guess is fine because I like palm trees just the way they are. But here it's sort of dynamic. Like every day you wake up and the weather's a little different, the light's a little different. It keeps you on your toes."

"That's my favorite part." We walked past the dorms and back toward the party. We could hear the muffled sounds of the band inside. Buddy stopped to sniff something, and we sat down on a bench to wait. This is the thing about walking a dog: You are really not on your own schedule at all. I wondered at the temperament of someone who could spend so much of his day at the whim of his dog's nose.

"You'd like L.A. The people are really easygoing."

"You're the only person I know from L.A., and you don't seem that easygoing."

"No kidding."

He laughed, and I opted to change the subject rather than

delve into exactly how easygoing I am not. "That could have been a really ugly scene in there. Thanks for helping me get her out. I could have let you finish the song, but I was losing my grip on her."

"She's the one losing her grip. It's got to be hard having a relationship like that blow up and then still having to see each other all the time."

"I think it's hard having a relationship blow up no matter where you are."

So far we had been in the safe side-by-side walking position that lends itself to a free flow of words without any pesky eye contact, followed by a side-by-side bench sit that also allowed us to watch the dog or our shoes. But now he looked at me, straight on. "Don't you have a boyfriend? The guy who was visiting that night?"

"Did. I haven't seen him since then."

"Oh. Sorry. What happened?"

"It's complicated."

Bass laughed and went to grab Buddy by the leash and bring him closer to us. "Complicated either means that you don't want to talk about it or you don't understand it."

"Both."

"Where does he live?"

"New York."

"That would be tough, anyway."

"That's what I keep hearing." Not only did I not want to think about John; I also did not want to rehash the ins and outs of why he may have broken up with me. Or whatever. "These days the only guy I'm interested in is Professor Halsey."

"That's unsettling."

"He's all I think about."

"He's eighty."

"I'm from L.A. I have an open mind."

I'M HAVING ANOTHER "IT SEEMED LIKE A GOOD IDEA AT THE TIME" MOMENT

TWO NIGHTS LATER I GOT TO meet Professor Halsey in person. It was Saturday night, and I dressed up like I was going on a date: new sweater, hair blown dry, lip gloss. Insane, I know. Danny had come to visit for the weekend but had a shockingly low amount of interest in nanoscience. The official reason for his visit was to check out Boston University, where my parents hoped he'd be accepted for the fall. But in the thirty-six hours since he arrived, he'd made no move to see the campus. I'd invited him to the lecture, but he'd declined, instead holding court with a bunch of girls on the main quad, roasting marshmallows on a hibachi and strumming his ukulele. All in a grass skirt and snow boots, of course. The girls thought he was adorable, and the setting sun and freezing temperatures didn't seem to bother them a bit. I had a feeling Danny was going to like college.

Professor Halsey was speaking at Building 4 about his hopes for expanding the Kavli Institute for Astrophysics and Space Research by publishing his recent studies on nanotechnology. Bass had the honor of introducing him and somehow managed to do so with dignity while wearing a T-shirt that said I HAVE CDO. IT'S LIKE OCD BUT ALL THE LETTERS ARE IN ALPHABETICAL ORDER LIKE THEY'RE SUPPOSED TO BE. Let's face it: If I could wear T-shirts with words, I would totally wear that one.

The fourteen audience members clapped at the end of the lecture. Only one of us actually stood up and cheered. All eyes were on me as I quickly sat back down and pretended to fish around in my bag. Everyone got up and approached the snack table and helped themselves to the small plate of Pepperidge Farm cookies and the gallon of iced tea. Whoever was in charge of snacks knew not to expect a big crowd.

I positioned myself between the podium and the table, so that Professor Halsey would have no choice but to acknowledge me if he wanted a Mint Milano. He looked down as he lumbered over with his cane, scanning the auditorium floor for unexpected hurdles. I weighed the risk of breaking his concentration by addressing him against the risk of losing my opportunity. All I could think of doing was spilling my whole plate of cookies on the floor in front of him. Well, at least he stopped.

"Hi, Professor!" I scooped up my cookies and offered him a crumby hand. He accepted it reluctantly. "I loved your talk. I've read everything you've ever written. I mean, not your personal correspondence or anything, but . . . I'm really . . . I was wondering . . . I'm Digit Higgins."

He narrowed his eyes with a little smile. "Ah, of course. The ambitious freshman who really wants that research job."

"I'm your biggest fan."

Bass made his way over to where we were standing to watch the show.

"So it seems. I had Sebastian here do a little research on you. It seems you were spotted riffling through my wastebasket. Campus Security thought I might have a stalker on my hands."

Um, yeah. I may have gone too far. "Stalker? I prefer science enthusiast." I shot Bass a help-me look.

The corners of his mouth turned up in a nano-smile. But I saw it. Halsey asked, "Don't you have something better to do on a Saturday night, something more fitting for a teenage girl?"

"My brother's visiting, and I said I'd take him to a party.

And I will, I swear. But I really just wanted to tell you, in person, how honored I would be if you considered my application for the job. I'd work really hard, and, as you can tell, I can get a little preoccupied with things I'm interested in."

"She's not easygoing, sir," Bass added.

Professor Halsey sighed. "Get me a Sausalito cookie, and you can come see me at eight a.m. on Monday morning. No promises, but we'll talk about it."

"Really?!" I leaned in to hug him and grazed his cane with my left leg, nearly sending him to the ground, where my cookie crumbs still sat. He steadied himself against Bass's arm and raised his free hand at me.

"Just get me the cookie."

"Sure. Sorry." I gave the professor a quick wave and caught Bass shaking his head like I was hopeless — which, at that moment, was the opposite of true.

I walked out into the vast expanse of Killian Court, victorious. Eight a.m. Monday morning! That job would be mine. I'd have access to all the nanotechnology research available at MIT. I'd dive into it. Swim in it. Add to it! I called Tiki, no answer. I called Danny, no answer. I'd tell them later — for the moment I was one giant leap closer to nanotechnology heaven. *Nerd-vana*, Danny might say.

I had a text from Bass:

> Clumsy execution but congratulations. You got your dream date! Coffee 7:30 Monday?
>
> Sure. Is it okay if I wear a T-shirt that doesn't say anything?
>
> I wouldn't. But feel free to take your chances.

I stood in the middle of a perfect square. Three sides were giant white buildings, and the fourth was the Charles River.

The three walls of buildings were numbered, not named, as if to remind me, unnecessarily, that this place was made for me. Building 10, wearing a huge dome for a hat, stood in front of me, flanked on either side by Buildings 1 through 8. These buildings stood like soldiers, perfectly symmetrical, with Buildings 7, 5, 3, and 1 to the left and 8, 6, 4, and 2 to the right. It was a standoff between an army of odd and an army of even. And although they were perfectly still, I could see how it would play out. Obviously the mighty even numbers adding up to 20 would topple the measly 16. But I admired those odd numbers for pairing up in such a way as to become even. The number 16 is balanced on two perfectly symmetrical 8s. Well done, Odd Army.

Killian Court is my happy place.

I turned back toward the Charles River and started walking home along Memorial Drive. But after three minutes, the euphoria wore off. It was nine o'clock and the sun had been down for over three hours. Streetlights projected shadows from the bare tree limbs like long crooked fingers. I suddenly had this creepy horror-movie feeling like there was a ghost in my underpants or someone was following me. I wondered if anyone besides Bass walked their dogs around here. I could really use a night watchman.

My boots sped up. I turned into Hayden Library to see if I could find Scott in his usual spot in the stacks and ask for an escort home. My whole body relaxed when I walked into the safety of the overheated building. I took the stairs down to the basement and walked to the very northwest corner of the section with the biology books. There was a hidden desk there that Scott thought gave him the power of mathematical clarity. I found his magic desk empty and made my way back to the stairs.

I heard footsteps again but ignored them. I remembered my terror of walking into the dark hallway on the first night in my dorm. This was no different, I told myself. The entire basement was completely deserted, and I would have seen anyone who was working in the stacks. Still, I stomped my boots harder than I normally would have, comforted by the strength of my own noise.

When the stairwell was three feet ahead of me, I picked up my pace because I felt the hairs on the back of my neck stand up. Moments later an arm wrapped itself around my neck. The body behind me was huge, with the right forearm acting as a vise and the bicep shoved in my right ear. That was all he needed to completely dominate me, a single arm. That, and the left hand that pressed a small pocketknife against my throat. I had seven dollars in my back pocket and wore my little gold necklace. This seemed like a lot of trouble to go to for a mugging. And what were the chances that he was waiting for some defenseless girl to walk down here on a Saturday night? The only explanation was that I'd been followed. They were tracking me. Adam Ranks's poster flashed in my mind.

"You don't want me." I squeaked the words out as his forearm crushed my windpipe. "The only guy I could identify has been caught. There's no reason to kill me. I have a job interview on Monday . . ."

His grip on my neck tightened and I struggled to get another breath. He growled, "Good news, little one. No one's going to kill you today. My orders are to keep you. Jonas Furnis wants you, and he wants you alive. No need for a job interview — we have an excellent job, and it's all yours. For as long as we let you live."

Terror. I'm not sure why being taken alive was so much scarier than being killed on the spot. "Job?" Sadness overcame my fear as I realized that I wouldn't make my Monday morning meeting. I thought of John hearing that I was missing. And my parents. And Danny out on the quad, clueless and happy. "Where are you taking me?"

"This is going to be easy." His hot breath flooded my ear. "We're going to climb up this flight of stairs and leave through the window I came in. Enjoy the fresh air when we get there, because you'll be working underground until you've completed your project." He laughed to himself. "And then I guess you'll just be underground." He was walking up the stairs now, slowly, with his forearm in place, pushing me ahead like a human shield.

I ran through my options, which were few. I had no weapon and no convenient kung fu training to fall back on. The window was a half flight of stairs ahead of us, and once we went through it, we were probably steps from a waiting car. The only advantage I had was that this thug had orders to keep me alive. And even if he disobeyed and slit my throat, it seemed better than being kidnapped.

So I lowered my chin, bit his forearm, and screamed when he loosened his grip on my neck in surprise. He pushed the knife in his left hand into my neck but stopped short of my windpipe. A floor above me, I heard a door fly open and the security guard call, "Who's down there?" I screamed again, and the knife slit the gash a little longer. I couldn't look down, but I could feel the blood dripping down my neck.

"I would have loved to have killed you." He whispered his hot breath in my ear. Frustrated, he threw me down the stairs and hurled himself through the open window.

It couldn't have been long before the security guard got to me and cradled my head in his arm. He was asking me my name and if I knew who hurt me. I turned away and curled up in a ball as it all came back to me, being chased by Jonas Furnis. The plane full of people who died due to my stupidity and the hundreds at Disney World whom I'd managed to help. I'd been kidding myself thinking that this was over. They'd been told I was dead. I was told they'd lose interest in finding me, anyway. That had seemed a little too neat to me, even at the time. But why now? Why hadn't they come for me months ago?

The security guard reached for his walkie-talkie to call an ambulance. I convinced him to bring me to his office upstairs first and to get me a bandage and some rubbing alcohol. I could tell the cut wasn't life threatening, and I'd been through this before. Plus I knew that as soon as I left this building, I'd be on the run.

He introduced himself as Officer O'Connell and eyed me suspiciously as I held his handkerchief to my wound. "Now, dear, if this was a fight with your boyfriend, there's no one who will win by your protecting him. You are going to have to let me call the police and get you to a hospital to be photographed. A pretty girl like you can do much better than barely getting away with her life."

"Sir, if you would please go one step further, I'm going to need you to call the FBI. I'll give you the number."

BOYFRIEND WANTED

JOHN WAS ON HIS WAY HOME for the night when he got the call on his cell phone. He gave Officer O'Connell instructions that I be kept in an interior room and was not to be left alone. He asked that no one be allowed to see me until he got there. Then he asked to speak to me.

"Uh, Miss Higgins, the gentleman from the FBI would like to ask you a few questions."

I wish I'd seen the look on his face when he heard this: "John, help me. It was them and they're back and they want to take me, to keep me. They want me to work with them and they know where I am and I'm going to have to go into hiding . . ." I was sobbing now. Hysterically. "I know you need your space or whatever, but I didn't know who to call. I can't go into hiding again — you were right, I need to be here. Okay. Okay . . . Hurry. Okay. Thanks."

When I handed the phone back to Officer O'Connell, his mouth was wide open. "Are you with the FBI?"

It actually seemed like the easiest answer. "Yes, and I cannot discuss our case any further." I wiped my face on the back of my sleeve. It was my new gray cashmere sweater with the fashion-forward (for me) navy cuffs, now with a snot-smeared sleeve. Nice way to reunite with my ex-boyfriend.

+ - +

John arrived four hours later and hugged me for too long. "When is this going to end?" he asked.

"It ended. You ended it. And I know I was harsh, but . . . Oh, you mean that. With them. I don't know." I should really teach a class on taking an ordinary awkward situation and turning it into a mortifying one.

He took a step back and smoothed the front of his suit jacket, remembering Officer O'Connell. "Yes, I'm glad to see you are okay. And you must be Officer O'Connell. Thank you so much for the critical role you played here tonight." I smiled a little as John showed him his badge and they shook hands. "The FBI will be taking over the investigation of this matter. I drove here as soon as I got the call."

Officer O'Connell seemed a little excited. "Okay, so I'm not going to contact the campus police. I'll just let you handle your, er, colleague here. Are you hungry? Want coffee?"

We both said that we'd love a coffee. It was almost two a.m., an odd time for coffee, but who knew when we'd sleep again? We'd be on the run, cooking food over an open fire in the woods.

"Danny's here." Terror overcame me again as I remembered that Danny was out there, maybe waiting for me in my dorm, but more likely still out on the quad roasting marshmallows. He'd be the easiest person to capture, if they wanted something to use against me.

John turned to Officer O'Connell. "Miss Higgins's brother is here visiting the campus. He is in danger and needs to be brought here for his own protection."

I was busy dialing his number. Miraculously, he answered. "Digit! You got any coconuts?"

"Listen to me. Are you still on the quad?"

"Sure, the hibachi's feeling a little weak, so we're gonna start a bonfire. Go big or go home, right, Dig?"

"Stay where you are. A security guard is going to come and get you and bring you here. We're in danger."

Officer O'Connell took out a pad of paper and licked the end of his pencil. "Can you give me a description?"

"Yeah, he's seventeen, desperately needs a haircut, and is probably the only guy out there in a grass skirt."

As soon as we were alone, John led me by the hand to the couch. It felt so strange to have him touch my hand, like that touch was some sort of tactile window into something I was trying to forget. I pulled my hand away to save myself. He took the bandage off my neck to inspect my wound, then rebandaged it carefully. He inspected my face. "So, hi," he said.

"Thanks for coming."

"Thanks for calling." Silence. "I don't think I can handle this again," he said.

"Just to be clear, we're talking about the whole attacked-by-terrorists thing, right?" I asked.

He nodded.

"Me either."

"How have you been?" he asked.

Sad, heartbroken, ecstatic about school, lost. "Fine."

"That's good." He took my hand again, searching it like the answer to this ongoing mess was in my lifeline. He put it down. "Sorry."

Sorry? Huh. For breaking my heart? That I almost got killed? Oh, for holding my hand. My mind was flipping between these two tragedies, the sliced neck and the broken heart, not really knowing which one I was reacting to.

"We need help." *Couples counseling? No, the thing with the terrorists.* I was starting to get it. "Let me check in with the FBI and let them know where I am." He was robot John again, all business. Pacing with his phone, he said, "I'm in Cambridge, Massachusetts. I had a call about an attack on a former FBI witness and came to investigate. No, I received the call directly. Because we had a personal relationship . . ." *Had. Nice.* He turned his body completely away from where I was sitting. "Yes, that same one. Yes. I am going to stay to get her to safety, maybe the Boston Bureau? Sure. Then I'll be back in

New York." He hung up and turned around. His face was pure pain. He came and sat next to me again.

"So, how's work?" I asked.

"Digit, it's crazy that we don't talk. I've been . . ."

Officer O'Connell cleared his throat as he came back in with our coffees and Danny.

"Jeez, Digit. What now?" Danny asked it like my habit of attracting bad guys was starting to get on his nerves. "And what are you doing here?"

John got up and shook his hand, explaining what had happened. Danny immediately tuned in to the bandage on my neck and came to take John's seat on the couch, strangely careful not to bend the grass on the back of his skirt. "Did you get a good look at the guy?"

I shook my head. I'd seen his big hairy forearm and remembered that it tasted salty when I bit it. I'd heard his voice, but a voice isn't necessarily easy to describe, especially if your brain isn't in its normal state. "All I know is that he was ordered to keep me alive and wanted to take me to work on some sort of project with them."

"My dad was worried about this." John started pacing the length of the room. "At first he was sure that the CIA was going to try to convince you to quit school and come work for them. He knew you wouldn't, but they can be pretty persuasive."

"Uh, yeah. I think I've been held at gunpoint and knifepoint enough times in the past year to know I don't want to make a career of it."

"He also said that when he started to understand your gift, he was worried about what it would mean if you were somehow under the control of the wrong people."

"What? Like someone would use my crazy mind as a weapon?"

"Yeah. And I think that's exactly what this was about tonight. If they'd wanted to punish you, he would have just slit your throat and taken off."

I shuddered. He was right. "So what now?"

"I take you in. When you're ready, I'm going to take you to the Boston Bureau."

Well, thanks, it's been nice catching up.

"I'm going to stay. Don't look at me like that. You have no clue what this has been like for me . . ."

John stopped talking when the door swung open. *Who the hell was this?*

From a million miles away, I heard Danny whistle. "Helloooo, Barbie."

DON'T MAKE ME RELEASE THE
FLYING MONKEYS

A YOUNG WOMAN, MAYBE TWENTY-FOUR, STOOD IN the doorway. I would have guessed that she was FBI if she didn't look so *CSI*. And by that I mean those ridiculously attractive actresses on the show with their suits tailored to highlight their long legs as they walk. Tiny steps, only tiny steps. She was tall, a personal pet peeve of mine, and naturally blond. (Don't get me started on natural blondes. You know they don't even have to shave, right?) And, okay, I've met tall blondes before but none that walked over to hug John and then stood with her hand cupping his elbow. For the second time tonight, alarm bells were ringing in my head. My survival instincts had kicked in bigtime.

John saw me eyeing her. "Oh, I'm sorry. Farrah, this is Spencer Frost." *What?!*

"Spencer? Your buddy from the Terror Task Force? And the gym?" I was trying to stay calm, but my voice was shaking a little. *And, P.S., Farrah?* He hadn't called me that since the day he'd heard the nickname Digit. Except for the day at the FBI when he left me. *Oh, God, would someone please take the kick-me sign off my back?*

"Hi, Farrah! Such a cute name! I'm so glad to finally meet you! I've spent so much time with John over the past few months, I've heard all about his old girlfriend!"

"Nice to meet you." I extended a hand that was attached to a snot-stained sleeve.

John wouldn't meet my gaze. "Spencer, what are you doing here?"

She was touching the sleeve of his suit with her perfectly manicured hand. Where were her cuticles? Do natural blondes not have cuticles? "I need to talk to you in private." *Uh, who doesn't?*

John looked left and right, as if to point out that we were in a small enclosed space with no screened-off private area. "What?" He was definitely agitated. "Why are you here?"

She led him a few feet away from us, not once taking that hand off his arm. "I was in the Boston Bureau and Bergen called me. He says you're on some unauthorized personal assignment and thinks it's best to have a third party involved in the situation. I'll take her from here." *Take your hand off his arm or the situation is going to get ugly.*

"Why were you even in Boston?"

"Training. Starts Monday."

What more could a girl ask for? I had an ex-boyfriend who'd been spending all of his time with Malibu Barbie, a brother who was dressed in drag, a slice across my neck, and a one-way ticket into witness protection.

"We can both take her into the Boston Bureau." John wasn't going to give up control of this situation, thank God.

Danny pulled John into a space of false privacy and whispered, "Listen, man, I get the space thing. But don't mess with her, okay. Just get her out of this and then leave her alone. Cool?" *Hello, I'm sitting right here.*

"If she doesn't want to discuss what happened with me, I'm not going to discuss it with you. But no one's going to hurt her."

Barbie herself was on the phone again, jabbering about my well-being. She was assuring the people at the FBI that I was okay and that she'd bring me straight to the Boston Bureau to try to identify the offending forearm in a photo.

Spencer got off the phone and pulled out a voice that should be reserved for talking to puppies. "So, tell me everything. How do you like being a big freshman?"

"Fine. We're mostly the same size as the seniors."

"Oh, I didn't mean that. It's just that college seems like forever ago to me. But it must be great for you here. I know it's hard for girls like you to connect with people in high school." Her phone rang and maybe saved her life.

As she paced around, John and I both watched her walk. I was trying to activate the dormant lasers that lived behind my eyes, in case I had any. I'm not sure what John's excuse was.

"I'm calling my dad." John got up and resumed his pacing as soon as Mr. Bennett answered. "Dad, I need help. They came after Digit—she barely got away. No. Not the National Security Agency. Jonas Furnis. Wait. Why?" His head came up slowly and his eyes met mine. "She's a college student, a kid. Sorry, not a kid, but come on. She's never . . . Fine. Hang on." John put the phone to his chest. "Digit, can you give me any reason in the world why the NSA may want you for questioning about espionage?"

Oh shit. "I can explain."

"Oh." He just shook his head and resumed his call. "Okay, I believe you. What do you want me to do? Okay. Okay. Just stall them and see what you can do. If the FBI wants to protect her and the NSA wants to question her, someone's going to have to make some decisions."

As John got off the phone, I prepared myself. It was a pretty simple explanation. I'd just start at the beginning, with the Facebook thing. From where I was sitting, this whole thing was Howard's fault. John had a different approach. "You hacked into the Department of Defense?!"

"Well, in a sense, yes."

It turns out that John can raise his voice. I'd only heard it once before, the time when we were hiding and he found out I'd brought my easily trackable phone with me. "I gave you your freedom so that you could save the world or whatever the hell it is you're supposed to be doing. And you go and hack into the DOD?"

"You gave me my freedom? Correction—you dumped me. You can't give someone freedom. This is America, John. I had my freedom already. Who do you think you are?" Weird, I guess I can raise my voice too. "So, yes, dumped but with the freedom that I already had, I hacked into the DOD."

"Now, Digit? Now you want to talk about this? After six weeks of no talking at all?" John seemed to become aware that we were shouting and airing our dirty laundry in front of everybody. He took a deep breath. "Okay. How 'bout you tell me why?"

"Fine. It wasn't to steal information. I mean, it was my information to have; they said I could have it. I had full authorization. I just needed it sooner, so I went in and took it." No one nodded in agreement or showed any signs of softening. I needed someone on my side. "Look. Danny. It's like when you're hungry for dinner and Mom's already made the Tater Tots. They're just sitting on the counter, but she's on the phone and hasn't served them yet. Your Tater Tots are just sitting there, see? And you're hungry. Those are your Tater Tots, so you just take them. I was going to miss a toga party, so I just went in a bit early and took what I needed. Like the Tater Tots."

"A toga party? Are you just making stuff up now?" John threw his hands up in the air.

Danny let out a slow whistle. "The NSA must really love those Tater Tots."

SMILE. THE GOVERNMENT IS WATCHING

As I EXPLAINED MYSELF IN THESE simple and irrefutable terms, John's face got whiter and whiter. He asked Officer O'Connell to please excuse us for a moment. As soon as he was gone, the pacing began. "Are you kidding me? You hacked into the DOD. You could be sitting in prison right now. I'm surprised you even got this far without them throwing you in jail. It's taken them two days to figure this out. They have got to be pissed. Oh my God." John's reaction was starting to clue me in to the fact that this may have been a bigger deal than I thought.

Spencer was calm, which made sense because she had nothing to lose from my being locked up forever. She could just give a little "tsk, tsk," escort me to the slammer, and continue to tantalize my ex-boyfriend with her fair and lanky ways.

"It's not like I stole state secrets. I just got the information I was going to get at eleven p.m. but earlier. It was a timing difference. Like Tater Tots."

"You're going to have to drop the Tater Tot defense. Those laws don't apply in this state," Danny said. He was shredding the grass on his skirt to improve its thickness.

John ignored him. "You hacked into the Department of Defense?" Seemed like we were in a game of Ping-Pong here.

"To get information I was going to get anyway. Yes."

"My dad is trying to protect you, putting his reputation on the line. He has some sort of unnatural faith in you." John stopped pacing. "He's trying to run interference, but I don't see how he's going to defend this."

I thought about Mr. Bennett and how he'd always been on my side. I'd missed seeing him and talking to him since the big breakup, and I had actually been a little surprised that he hadn't contacted me. My relationship with John had always seemed sort of secondary to him. He treated me like a peer, with an unwavering admiration for my abilities. He seemed to think that their applications were far beyond even what my dad hoped for, which made me feel good and nervous at the same time. Even though things with John were up in the air, I knew Mr. Bennett would always have my back.

John sat down next to me, but a million miles away. I racked my brain for something to say until finally Barbie's phone rang and broke the silence.

"Spencer Frost. Oh, hi. Yes, I'm here with them. Yes, of course she's here. What? The director? Of the CIA? When did he get involved? Sure, I'll hold. Hello, sir. Yes, I heard." Listening. "Oh, my. Well, yes, sir. Will do." Spencer hung up the phone and plopped into the metal chair behind the officer's desk. This choice of seating, combined with how useless the rest of us were being, made her seem completely in charge.

She addressed John. "It seems he wants her brought directly to Langley."

"Why is the CIA even involved in questioning someone accused of hacking? I thought the NSA was dealing with this. There's no international component to this." He turned to me. "Or do you have a European accomplice you're just waiting for the right time to tell us about?"

I confess I made a face at him that I would normally reserve for Danny. "Very funny. No."

Spencer again controlled the conversation. "Well, first of all, because the NSA no longer wants her for questioning. She is now under arrest for felony espionage. That was the director of the CIA himself on the phone. He has made himself personally involved and is moving the investigation to the CIA. He seems very angry and used a few choice words that I won't repeat. He doesn't want her talking to anyone. He says to bring her in and that they'll deal with her at the Farm."

John was intrigued. "Is that exactly what he said? About the Farm?"

"Well, I took out the expletives, but, yes, he said the Farm; he wants her at Langley ASAP."

John just stared at Spencer. When he was done, he stared at the floor. Back to Spencer, then a little floor time . . . not once did he look at me.

"Is there still time for John's dad to help me? How did this move from questioning me to arresting me so fast? Why is he so mad, anyway?"

John said to no one, "You've got to be kidding me. Listen, my dad can fix this. Especially if it's being handled by the CIA now. He knows the director and can explain to him about how harmless, if misguided and stubborn, Digit is. He just has to do it before this gets any media attention. Let me call him back." John tried his dad's cell. There was no answer, so he tried his mom. He apologized for calling so late, made a few seconds of small talk, and asked to speak to his dad. "He's away on assignment? Where? I wish you knew too." John immediately called his dad's office at the CIA, where his assistant picked up at three a.m. "Yeah, hey, sorry you're there so late. Do you know where my dad is? Vacation? With my mom?"

John hung up the phone and ran his hands through his hair a few times, studying the floor again. "He can't help us. I don't know where he is or what he's doing."

Spencer decided to take over. "I am going to help you." She straightened her back and placed all ten of her perfect fingers on the table. "Listen, John. Digit. Can I call you Digit?" *No.* I nodded. "It sounds like we need to buy ourselves a little time until Henry can work his magic." *Henry? How is he Henry to you and Mr. Bennett to me?* "What you did was absolutely illegal, but innocently intentioned. We need to wait and see if Henry can get you out of this before the CIA gets their hands on you. I'll phone in and say we are leaving for Langley now. But we'll take the scenic route."

Mix your emotions much? In one breath Spencer calls my Mr. Bennett by his first name and tells me that she is going to defy the orders of the FBI and the CIA to help me evade arrest. I had the strangest urge to hug her. With something sharp.

She got out of her chair and perched across from me on the security desk. She didn't need the height advantage to intimidate me. "You really must be as smart as John says. It's just amazing. I'm curious to know, how did you hack into their system?"

"It's hard to explain."

"Nothing's hard for you to explain, Dig." Danny seemed like he just wanted this to be over. There were coconuts to be had.

I looked up at Spencer and found her waiting. Her perfect green eyes, her blond but not too blond eyebrows slightly raised. I swear I was going to spill it, just outline for her exactly how I got in. She said she'd help me after all, and John seemed to trust her, and I was just so tired. But as I started to speak, my eyes fell to where her lovely hands rested on her hairless thigh. And I asked myself: *How am I ever going to be able to compete with a woman who has this little body hair?* Answer: *I cannot.* All I had going for me was the wacky math brain. I wasn't going to share any of it.

"It's weird, this thing that happens to me. It's like I see a math problem or something and my mind just starts calculating, but I kinda black out. When I've gotten to the answer, or in this case cracked the passwords and accessed the mainframe, I don't remember how I did it. Sorry."

Danny narrowed his eyes at my lie. He knew I could talk all day about how I solved a problem. And John, maybe reading my mind, tried to hide the tiniest smile.

"That wasn't my understanding." Spencer got up to take her turn pacing.

At four a.m. we left the library and dashed to Spencer's car. She and John sat in the front; Danny and I sat in the back. Just like when we were kids. "This is what it'd be like if Mom and Dad worked for the FBI," he whispered. "Except Mom's kinda hot." This must have hit a raw nerve in my fist because it punched him hard in the arm.

At Logan Airport, we pulled up to Budget Rent A Car and switched to a navy blue Honda four-door. Spencer had this all figured out. We were going to say we'd been followed and had to switch cars, and that we'd had to go into hiding for a few days to be sure we lost them.

We checked into the airport Hilton to get exactly five hours of sleep before we started our run. I bought myself a toothbrush, a ChapStick, a razor, and tweezers in the lobby store, knowing these would be my only beauty staples for the foreseeable future. Spencer wheeled her undoubtedly well-stocked overnight bag to the registration desk and paid for two rooms in cash. She handed one key to John. "You can share with Danny, and I'll bunk with Digit. She is my responsibility after all." *Evil genius.*

John and I went our separate ways, without a word.

At eleven a.m., we all met in the hotel restaurant to dig in to the dregs of the breakfast buffet. Spencer was fresh as a daisy in neatly pressed khakis and a fitted white blouse. I was in the clothes I'd slept in. Plus ChapStick.

Danny was completely disoriented, not having had his customary twelve hours of sleep, but he seemed to have showered and re-donned his grass skirt and snow boots.

"Seriously, Danny. It's time to lose the skirt."

"All I've got under it are boxers. The skirt stays."

I guess I hadn't noticed he wasn't wearing any pants under

there. "Well, weren't you freezing last night? How can you go outside without pants?"

"That's why I was going to build a bonfire, Dig." Danny leaned over and grabbed my left earlobe in the most annoying possible way. "Listening. Ever try it?"

John agreed. "Right?"

When Danny and Spencer hit the buffet, John grabbed my hand to keep me behind. "Hey. I know we need to talk."

Uh, hello, understatement. "Yeah. And there's a lot you didn't tell me about Spencer." *Like she has ovaries.*

"I know." Not exactly what I was hoping for. "We've got to get in touch with my dad again. He really picked the wrong time to disappear."

Spencer and Danny came back with plates of fresh-ish fruit and breakfast meats, respectively. Spencer picked up a strawberry and smiled with pleasure like it was a donut. I asked, "Have you tried his cell this morning?"

"Six times. But he won't answer. He's obviously doing something he doesn't even want my mom to know about. He's not going to pick up the phone."

Danny said, "Just send him a text and tell him we're in trouble. Or that Digit's screwed up even worse than he thought, to be more exact." Danny had turned talking while chewing into an art form.

"I did. I texted 911 last night. No word." Just then his phone vibrated on the table. "It's him. 'I'm in 911 too. Can't involve you without danger. Don't leave Digit's side. Stop calling.' Oh my God."

"We've got to find him." I resisted the temptation to grab John's hand.

"He said not to." John looked totally hopeless.

"Listen, he doesn't want you to find him because he doesn't want you in danger. But he's in danger. And if we can't find him, I'm going to jail."

"Digit, he could be anywhere. And if he doesn't want to be found, he won't be. That's his job."

Spencer piped up, "Yes, this isn't like a lost puppy where we can go around the neighborhood calling his name, sweetie."

I'm. Not. Six.

"What phone did he text you from?"

"His personal phone, his iPhone."

"Who's his carrier?" I grabbed my laptop and headed back up to my room. As the elevator doors closed, I heard Danny call after me, "Try not to black out too bad, Dig."

It's easier than you think to hack into Verizon's customer database and locate a phone that's been accessing the Internet or sending a text. It took me ten minutes to locate Mr. Bennett in central West Virginia. Afterward I showered, shaved my legs, and painstakingly blew dry my hair to kill a little extra time. Blackouts aren't quick.

No one was surprised when I came back to the restaurant and announced that I'd found him. John said there was no way he was going to drive me directly into more danger. Spencer said there was no way to avoid it. Danny said that a good road trip calls for a lot of snacks.

HONK IF YOU DO EVERYTHING
YOU'RE TOLD

MY SECOND TRIUMPH OF THE DAY was getting Danny to call shotgun so that John and I could be alone in the back. This seemed to annoy Spencer, which was my third triumph of the day.

It's a thirteen-hour drive from Boston to central West Virginia. Our destination seemed to please Spencer, and for the first time I started to see her as an FBI agent. She was decisive and stuck to her plan. She was pleased that we were driving right toward Virginia — where the FBI thought we were headed — so that our story about being followed on our way there checked out. She also knew of someplace where we could spend the night in New River, West Virginia, and in the morning we would try to determine where Mr. Bennett might be hiding, or where he might be held captive. I'll admit the plan was a little loose, but it effectively got me out of where Jonas Furnis thought I was and got me closer to someone who might be able to fix things for me with the CIA.

The vibe between John and me wasn't really changing. I guess we needed to have some big conversation, but this was hardly the place for it. He'd seemed very angry about me not wanting to talk for so long. And I had wanted to talk. I mean, I had wanted to talk to him. But I just hadn't wanted to talk the whole thing through. Needing space feels like leaving, and everyone knows you can't go backwards in a relationship. I guess I just didn't want to hear him dump me again.

We each sat by a window in the back seat, leaving the middle seat as no man's land, not to be crossed. After a few hours I pulled my knees into no man's land, stealing more space for myself but still not touching John. The trees changed along the highway as we made our way south. Nearly every highway was lined with some sort of thin forest on either side, probably to protect the nearby houses from the noise. I thought about my perfectly landscaped street in Santa Monica and the fig tree in the front yard. A team of six men descend on our house to care for that tree and the rest of our small yard every week. They trim in the fall and prune in the spring, even fertilize a few times a year to really stink things up. I didn't see any landscapers on the sides of the highways; these trees seemed to take care of themselves. And they looked no worse for it.

Of course, there was starting to be a really good chance I'd have the opportunity to sport a bright orange jumpsuit along one of these highways, picking up garbage and sweeping acorns out of the road. Call me a little stressed out, but that actually sounded kind of relaxing.

Somewhere around Pennsylvania, John took my hand. I tried not to move. He traced the back of it, like it was some mysterious new object. I watched his face looking at my hand for the longest time. When my throat started to close up and I thought I might start to cry, I shut my eyes and pretended to sleep. He kept holding my hand.

Spencer's phone had been ringing since we got into the car. On the sixth hour of our drive, she decided to pick it up. "Hey. Yeah. We've run into some trouble. We were followed on our way out of Boston and had to hide out for the night." She paused and moved the phone slightly away from her head as the volume of her boss's voice escalated. "Yes, I understand that she's a threat now, but if they get their hands on her, we've got a national emergency." I'd take a compliment any-where I could, but I'm not sure I wanted that one. "We're taking the scenic route, and we'll get there as soon as we can. Okay? So, otherwise are things good? How's little Sophie?" She looked at the phone in her hand, as if it would tell her why her boss had just hung up on her.

My mouth opened and this came out: "Thanks, Spencer." I mean, she was lying to her boss to help save my butt. It was certainly unexpected.

She let out a little laugh. "Sure. Any friend of John's is a friend of mine." And now I hated her again.

We didn't stop to eat until after nine p.m. at an old din-er outside of Morgantown, West Virginia. At first glance it looked like one of those diners that was built inside an aban-doned train car. But upon closer examination, I could see that it was really an old Greyhound bus remodeled to look like an old train. All this deception was getting to me.

We sat down and ordered. John got a cheeseburger, I got a Mexican omelet, Danny got the Lumberjack Special, and Spencer got a scoop of chicken salad. On a bed of lettuce but not iceberg. Did they have a darker lettuce, maybe arugula they could use? Dressing? Of course not.

"What, are you like a rabbit?" Danny asked.

"Rabbits don't eat chicken," Spencer explained.

"Right. You know who can eat chicken? Digit! Dude, have you ever seen her attack a rotisserie chicken? It's like some-thing from the Nature Channel!"

John choked on a bit of water, laughing. "Yeah, I've seen it. But what about a chili cheeseburger? It's like a week's worth of food, and she can put it away in three bites."

Spencer's eyebrows were high. Mortified for me, it seemed. What's wrong with having an appetite? "Yes, I eat. Sue me. I'm going to the bathroom."

John snapped back to attention and stood up, wiping his mouth with his napkin. "Hey, I'll take you."

Spencer nudged him. "God, John, she'll be fine. They haven't followed us; they have no clue where we are. It's a diner. She'll be fine." And then John took the most awkward pause. Looking back and forth between us, choosing, and then finally sitting down and nodding.

I stood there for a moment not knowing what to do. Was I disappointed that he wasn't going to follow me to the bathroom? Or because she made light of my predicament and he agreed with her?

I walked down past the bar to the ladies' room sign that was really a personalized license plate from Hawaii: LADEEZ. A train, a bus, and now a Hawaiian car? This place could make me nuts. I pushed in the door to the restroom and had all of the air knocked out of me. It was a quick jolt to my gut as a strong arm pulled me inside and then a firm handkerchief to the mouth with the other arm. I could feel the strength of my assailant and knew I was outmatched by a factor of six.

"Shhh. No one hears you. Clear?" I knew the voice, but how was that possible? "Don't move. We need to talk." His hands released from my gut and my mouth, and he spun me around.

"Mr. Bennett? Jeez, you hurt me." I rubbed my belly where I'd just had the Heimlich maneuver to end all Heimlich maneuvers. Then I threw my arms around him. "Oh my God, John's going to be so glad we found you! I did something really stupid, which of course you know about, and I'm in so much trouble: They want to arrest me for felony espionage, plus the nuts are after me again and they attacked me but they don't want to kill me—they want to keep me because I'm some sort of national threat, and I got an interview for the job I really want but it's tomorrow and we are so far away from school that it's never going to happen . . ."

"Can you calm down? I don't have a lot of time, but I have a lot to say, and John can't see me."

"Okay." I took a deep breath and looked up at him. I swear

he's like God: big and strong and just magically there reading your mind whenever you need him to be.

"I've been tracking you since last summer."

My heart raced in ten directions. *Tracking me? Like when? Like when I was alone with John? Like then? Oh my God.*

The mind reader's smirk creeped up. "No, not like that. I mean that I've just kept tabs on you, through your computer activity. I know it's a bit of an invasion of your privacy, but I didn't know any other way to make sure that you were okay. At first I thought I could just have John do it, but he accused me of being 'unnaturally interested' in your relationship. And then the thing happened with you two." He rolled his eyes. "When I'm traveling, my assistant does the monitoring. I figured that if I could confirm that you were on your laptop every day doing normal student things, then I would know you were okay. And if you missed a day, I'd come looking. The interesting part was that I could tell someone else was tracking your computer activity. I suspected it was Jonas Furnis but couldn't prove it. And the two of us have been watching you, side by side, for months. But when I saw you hack into the DOD, I knew the NSA would see it and that they weren't the only group that would want you in their custody. Jonas Furnis has money now, Digit, and if they had you, they'd be deadly."

"They were broke, remember? Where are they getting money?" I'd never heard of rich people holding fundraisers for terrorists.

He didn't answer me. "I found Jonas Furnis."

"Where?"

"Their headquarters. You wouldn't believe it. But one man can't take them down. I need to get a whole assault team to go down there. After somehow explaining why I was there while saying I was on vacation. Jonas Furnis knows I've infiltrated by now; they have surveillance everywhere. I need to get out of here. I neutralized one of their operatives and took this from him. Keep it for me in case I don't make it back to

D.C. It proves what they are doing." He tossed me an HP 12C, a standard run-of-the-mill financial calculator, a little bigger than my iPhone and a lot less interesting.

"Why would I ever need this?" *I mean, c'mon.*

"You'll see. Now I've got to go."

"Hang on." I grabbed the sleeve of his jacket. "What are we supposed to do? And why can't I tell John?"

"Pretend you never saw me. Go back out there, say nothing. I'm better off alone without you guys leading them to my door. Wander around the countryside while I get back to headquarters. I need to be the one to tell the director of the CIA about what you did. He can help run interference with the NSA."

"He already knows. He's pissed and he's taken over the investigation."

Mr. Bennett was quiet. "Why wouldn't he have called me? He knows you and I are practically family. Never mind. They'll do anything I want when they find out I've found Jonas Furnis. I'll get them to leave you alone. I'm building us a little street cred, like you kids say." *We don't say that, by the way.* "I need time." He turned to go again but stopped. "You okay?"

"Not really. There's this girl."

"Impossibly blond and put together? We've met her."

"I can't believe he's gone for someone so tall and blond and without hair follicles. He never takes his eyes off her. What am I supposed to do?" I was holding on to my already dirty sleeves and wiping my tears again.

"Use your head, Digit." He lifted my chin up to eye level. "Stay focused. I've got big plans for you, as always." He hoisted himself out of the bathroom window.

So she'd met his parents? I shoved the calculator in my back pocket and took a minute to splash water on my red eyes.

WARNING: I HAVE CABIN FEVER

~

IT WAS THE MIDDLE OF THE night when the car stopped abruptly, and I woke up with my face pressed into the door handle and my boots on John's lap. "We're heeeere," Spencer chirped. We got out of the car and stepped into the pitch-black night. Spencer walked ahead, unlocked a door, and flipped on the light of a tiny cabin.

Inside, I plopped down my backpack, and it seemed to take up half the living space. And the dining space. I saw blankets stacked in the corner and realized this was also the sleeping space.

"Like it?" Spencer beamed. "My family and I used to spend summers in this cabin. So many memories." *Where do you keep them?*

"Oh-kay." Danny looked around. "I think I might still be asleep — where can I crash?"

Spencer motioned to the blankets and we all claimed our spots. Danny collapsed onto his blanket right where he stood. Spencer positioned herself horizontally in front of the door, my hero. John laid his stuff out next to mine.

Lights out. "Digit? You okay?" John whispered.

I thought: *Not really. I've just flushed my life down the toilet and am lying down next to my old boyfriend who can't stop star-ing at a girl I can't compete with.* I said, "Not really. I've just flushed my life down the toilet and am lying down next to my old boyfriend who can't stop staring at a girl I can't compete with."

"Can we talk about this later?" Yeah, sure. I'm pretty sure visiting hours at Sing Sing are Thursdays from two to six.

I turned my back to him and pretended to go to sleep. I was wide awake, fuming. I imagined tearing into Spencer with exactly the right insult and storming off to leave behind only the memory of my quick wit and sharp tongue. I got taller as I walked away, so tall actually that she came to fear me. But really, what was there to tear apart? Her beauty? Her willingness to delay my imprisonment? Her self-control around salad dressing?

Regressing back to the fourth grade, I started playing with my new calculator. Typing 7734 and turning it over to read the word HELL. Amateurish. I tried to spell GO TO HELL SPENCER in numbers but got stuck on the G. I typed a 5 for an S and accidentally hit the Enter button with my pinkie. The calculator started to vibrate, silently, and I just held on not knowing what I was waiting for.

All of a sudden, a piece of paper emerged from the left side, slowly, like it was coming out of an ink-jet printer. I could barely see it in the dark room, but the feel of the paper was familiar and unmistakable. I reached into my backpack to pull out my phone and shone a little light on it. It was a five-dollar bill.

For fun, I pressed 20 Enter. *Vibrate, vibrate,* twenty-dollar bill. I pressed 100 Enter. *Vibrate, vibrate,* one-hundred-dollar bill. I'd just made $125. I ducked my head under my blanket and turned on the flashlight app on my phone. In the brighter light, the bills looked absolutely real, including the 3-D overlay of the metallic eagle on the twenty-dollar bill. I remembered reading that, besides the linen paper, that eagle image was the thing that kept amateur counterfeiters out of business. The change in ink and printing process of that 3-D overlay made dollar bills nearly impossible to replicate.

Where did Mr. Bennett get this money machine? I sat straight up as it hit me. Jonas Furnis has money now. And they have money because they have Adam Ranks.

"What the . . . ?" Evidently my eureka moment had sent my backpack, laden with my laptop, flying over to John's make-shift bed. He sat up too, rubbing his arm where he'd been hit.

"Shhh. Come under here." I checked to see that everyone else was sleeping and scooted over to make room for John under my blanket. Half asleep, he moved over to lie next to me, scooping his arm around me like it was the most normal thing in the world. I lay there for a second, smelling the John smell of his T-shirt and feeling the John feel of his shoulder underneath my head. It was a stolen moment, a cheap thrill at the expense of a sleeping man, but I'd take it. Because I was about to fess up to another lie.

"So I saw your dad," I whispered into his chin.

"I know you love him, Digit. We'll find him. Tell me about your dream tomorrow." He was more than half asleep.

I whispered an inch from his ear, "I mean, I saw him for real, at the diner. He told me not to tell you, said that we needed to keep roaming around to buy him time to defend me. He's found Jonas Furnis. He said they have money. And I know how they're getting it."

All systems were go. "You saw my dad? Is he okay?"

"Shhh. He's making his way back to Langley. He gave me this." I pressed the calculator into his hand. "Name a meal you really enjoyed."

"Okay, osso buco in Boston. The last meal I had before the silence started."

"How much did it cost?"

"I don't know, maybe a hundred dollars?"

I typed 100 and Enter, and out it came, a hundred dollars. "We're even." John ran his fingers over the bill and held it up to the light of my phone.

I explained about the calculator and what it did. "And the reason everybody isn't counterfeiting all the time is that the 3-D overlay is so hard to do. But Adam Ranks knows how to do it. They have him, and he's given them this technology."

John kept running his finger over the new bill in the dark. "If they could print endless money and had someone who could hack into the U.S. government's most secure divisions, they could take down the system. They could overthrow our government."

I pulled the blanket up over our heads so we were in our own cave. I whispered, "Which is exactly what the CIA thinks I'm trying to do anyway. Which is insane. I like the government and the roads and schools and stuff. Why would I ever mess with them?"

"Obviously, to go to a toga party." John still had his arms around me, as we lay staring at each other in the pitch-blackness. I had, as usual, a thousand things to say. All of them were going to make me vulnerable to having my heart ripped out again. John touched my face in a way that made me want to cry. "I can't tell if you're smiling or frowning," he said.

"Both."

"I know exactly how you feel."

Flashlights illuminated the room. I pulled our covers down to see what was going on and saw Danny sitting up, rubbing his eyes, and three men with guns surrounding us. Spencer was standing behind them so I figured they were the CIA or the FBI. Man, I'd really screwed up bigtime.

John jumped immediately to his feet but was knocked flat on his back by the butt of a rifle. "Hang on!" I grabbed the smallest guy by the arm. "He's with you guys. I'm the one that did the bad thing. Jeez, I'm coming."

"You're all coming. You'll come to work, and this guy and the clown in the skirt can come to die. Nice work, Spencer." The one in the middle gave her a little nod.

John got up, holding his stomach, and came to my side. Nothing made sense to me. Well, not until they bound our wrists with plastic handcuffs and marched us off to meet Jonas Furnis. Spencer gave her hair a little flip as I passed her.

Bitch.

TREE-HUGGING DIRT WORSHIPER

IT WAS A PRETTY SHORT DRIVE from Spencer's cabin to Jonas Furnis's place. I should have known that she wouldn't have spent summers in a crappy cabin like that. Stupid.

She rode up in the front of the van with her thug buddies, and John, Danny, and I sat on a long bench in the back. They stripped us of cell phones, laptops, and my new magic calculator. Danny looked like his world had been turned upside down. "You carry a calculator now?!"

"It's a money-printing machine; it's theirs."

"Nice move. Next time you get your hands on a money machine, stick it down your pants, will you?"

"At least I'm wearing pants." Danny looked a little vulnerable, cuffed in a grass skirt. It reminded me of the time he was cast as Mary in his second grade Christmas pageant. (This sort of thing only happens in Los Angeles.) "Danny, I'm so sorry. I'm so sorry you're here and part of this. So sorry you're not going to get to go to college and teach everyone at BU how to hula dance."

"It's okay, Dig. I wasn't going to college anyway."

"What? When did you decide that?"

"Forever ago. I just don't have the heart to tell Dad. I mean, he's Mr. College, but it's just not for me. I want to do things, not read about them. Like maybe I could be an electrician? Or a carpenter. Or an actor."

I looked at Danny and totally saw him as the love interest in any teen drama. He had the hair, the steady gaze, and the authentic coolness that would melt the audience. And he had great comedic timing, actually. "Acting, yeah, I could see that."

"Yeah, but you've got to help me talk to Mom and Dad. I mean, what could Mom say? She's an actress and she, like, breathes that stuff. But Dad . . ."

John snapped, "Uh, seriously, guys? Reality check? We're being marched to our deaths and possibly the death of our nation. How about this: If my dad gets back here soon enough to save us, I'll talk to your parents myself? Okay?"

Embarrassed, Danny and I shut up as asked. But shutting up can be so much work. I asked John, "So you knew about Spencer?"

"I suspected."

"But why?" Maybe suspicion of natural blondes was a universal thing?

"It was a lot of things. Her story about the director's reaction to your little crime seemed really out of character for him. He wouldn't have taken it personally; he's very pragmatic. He wouldn't have waited for you to get to Langley; he's very impatient. And he definitely wouldn't have cursed; he thinks foul language is a sign of a weak mind."

"How would you know all that about him?"

"He's my godfather."

Danny rolled his eyes.

John went on: "And the Farm? No one in the CIA, certainly not the director, would call Langley 'the Farm.' The Farm is an offsite training center for covert ops. They only call Langley the Farm in the movies. Everybody knows that."

"Everybody. Right." Danny looked at John like he was from a different planet.

The van stopped, and we were walked single file, me first, toward a long, low building. It was constructed log cabin style, but with an aluminum roof covered in polka dots. As we got closer to the building, the polka dots stopped me in my tracks. They were actually sculptures of butterflies, inlaid with small pieces of glass that reflected the light of the rising sun. They reflected every possible color of the rainbow, depending on their angle, and were arranged randomly. Each one looked as if it had just landed on the roof and was ready to take off again. Beautiful.

A voice from the doorway called to me, "They're made of solar panels, young Digit. Like them?" I looked toward the voice and saw a completely bald man, very thin and maybe in his early sixties, in jeans and a poncho. "Please come in. I'm Jonas Furnis. I'll be your host." All the thugs, including Barbie Thug, laughed at his joke.

The guns in our backs led us toward him. Jonas Furnis put his hands on my shoulders, maybe in lieu of shaking my bound hand. "Ah, Digit. You've caused us so much trouble. But now, now you are going to make it all better. In a matter of days, we will consider ourselves even. No hard feelings. Ready to get to work, or would you like to have a look around?"

Because I knew the get-to-work part of this story was probably going to end up as the *Torture Digit Show,* I asked to have a look around. Jonas took us into a small entryway that led to a square pool. Above the pool was a ten-foot-tall iron sculpture of a woman, whose hands reached up as if to support the ceiling. Water trickled through the bottoms of her feet into the pool. "It's our potable water system. Rainwater flows from the roof through Mother Earth's hands into the cistern. We have more than enough water for all of our needs. Come."

He walked us through a busy kitchen. Five people (and I mean normal people, not crazy goons bent on world destruction) washed glasses, squeezed juice, and carried baskets of eggs from the small coop outside. They looked peaceful in their work, if thrown back a bit in time.

Jonas led us outside and along the perimeter of the compound. The building had been constructed entirely of driftwood and fallen trees. It was insulated by old blue jeans that he'd found at the Salvation Army. All the metal and glass had been rescued from condemned buildings and repurposed to create a truly beautiful structure.

The compound sat on a quickly moving river, which provided constant hydro energy and food for the twenty-four people who lived there. He showed us the geothermal energy system that in the winter moved the heat from the earth into the building and in the summer moved the cooler air up. What wasn't provided by these energy sources came from the sun, via the butterflies. It was a completely off-the-grid, zero-impact, super-green haven. I was having a hard time remembering that I was there against my will.

"You see, we are living here peacefully and are taking nothing from Mother Earth that she does not want to give us freely." Jonas finished the tour of the ground floor in his office. John and I were each offered a seat, while Danny shifted nervously behind us, probably for the first time regretting the whole grass skirt look.

Jonas Furnis addressed John first. "You can stay as long as you don't speak. Nod to indicate that you understood me." John nodded, and Jonas turned his attention back to me. "Are you wondering why your government doesn't encourage this type of lifestyle for its citizens? Sorry, was I reading your complicated little mind?" *Kinda.* "It's because there's no money in it for them. They are so ingrained in their system, their outdated utilities, the tax revenue from manufacturing and selling plastic nonsense. They believe they need to keep raping Mother Earth to survive. And they think I'm sick!" Nods and chuckles from the thugs in the doorway.

His desk was an old wooden door balanced on two sawhorses. He had an assortment of maps and weather charts sprawled out as if we'd caught him during exam week. Perfectly squared to the upper-right-hand corner of his desk was a paperback copy of *Silent Spring*.

He caught me staring. "Have you read it?"

"I had to for AP Environmental Science."

"What did you think?" *Oh great, we're in a book club now.*

"I found it kind of depressing. But I know it made a big difference in your . . . in the environmental movement."

"It did. It made all the difference in the world. It's the only reason we have birds anymore. If you work quickly, I might let you read it again." He leaned back in his chair and placed both hands, decisively, on the table. "Now that I'm flush with cash, we are going to start fresh. And I mean you, me, and Mother Earth. Plus whoever else survives. There will be fewer people, and they will have no choice but to live off the earth in a cooperative way. When you're ready, we'll get started. You see what we're doing here?"

"No?"

"Have you ever seen *Little House on the Prairie*?"

Danny jumped in. "I totally love that show; it's on late night cable. I had the biggest crush on Mary, even when she went blind."

"My apologies. I forgot to tell you: You don't speak either."

"No, I have never seen it," I answered.

Danny threw his arms down in disbelief. I could hear his disappointment loud and clear: *How could you possibly not have seen* Little House on the Prairie? *It's classic television. You and your crazy math stuff that no one cares about . . .* I was half grateful that Danny wasn't allowed to speak.

"It's just an example, maybe familiar to a few night owls, of how people used to live with nature. They did not try to control it. When the sun went down, they slept. When the sun came up, they woke. Nature is here to control us, and we are best served to honor it and live within the boundaries it sets for us. You and I, Digit, we are going to give the earth back to Mother Earth. Once she is no longer under attack, she can get back to taking care of herself." I thought back to the trees by the highway, all surviving on their own. No pruning, no sprinkler system. "In doing so, we are going to give the human race back to itself. We are going to shut down all the noise of the modern world. If you want a toy, you can carve it out of wood. If you want entertainment, you can talk to another human being. Sick people will die, rather than being kept alive artificially, and they will leave room for new life. In this way we will control the population so that the burden placed on our Mother can be alleviated."

To be honest, I think the scariest part of this conversation was that he seemed like the sanest person in the world. I could totally see how his followers walked away from their lifestyles to embrace this. I had a thousand questions for him. How deeply did he think we'd already injured the earth? Did he really think people could be retrained to live that way? What if there was an outbreak of some horrible disease because there was no medicine? Would he let us move forward in time for a minute to produce some?

I only asked this one: "Why can't you just educate people? Can't you just spread your message? I mean, I feel like taking responsibility for what we are doing to the earth is stuff that most people can agree with."

He shook his head. "It's too late. Think of your veins, how they move blood through your body. You are a living organism. If someone threatened your life, you would fight back. The rivers are Mother Earth's veins. She is a living organism. She has been poisoned for so long that this is her time to fight back. I am here, sent as her soldier. She calls me the Guardian. We will eradicate much of what is killing her and allow a new world to prevail. After you are done, Digit, the U.S. government will be broke. I am building a new treasury just beneath where you are now sitting, and I will be the new government. Things will be done my way, her way."

Okay. Hmm. Less sane now. We'd gone a little off the rails. *She calls him the Guardian? Like when she speaks to him?*

"She told me that she would send me a squire. I waited for a long time, and when my work was foiled by a teenager, I knew that it could not be an accident. Squires, in more chivalrous times, were teenagers, you see. You, Digit, you are to be my squire. Mother Earth has brought us together as her warriors. We shall save her together."

Um, squire? "Um, squire?"

"Mother Earth whispered it to me years ago. She promised me a young helper. She told me again when I was in despair over our failure at Disney World. And I knew that she meant you when I saw the dozens of photos of trees you have on your laptop. In your heart, you are a friend of the earth."

"Yeah, I like trees. A lot. But mainly they're there because I'm . . ." I looked back in time to see Danny making a curlicue with his finger by his head to indicate that I am, in fact, cuckoo.

"Because you are my squire. I am the Guardian, knighted by Mother Earth, and you are my young squire. You will accept this truth, and we will be victorious."

Um, yeah, okay. But if you make me dress up in tights and armor and stuff, I'm gonna flip out.

Honestly, as maniacal as he seemed, I wasn't really that scared. John was sitting right next to me, and I knew that Mr. Bennett knew where we were and had gone to fetch an army. Add to that the fact that John realized that Spencer was a lying criminal (even worse than me!), and I actually felt okay. I'd been in worse spots for sure. All I had to do was act like some weirdo's squire, work as slowly as possible, and wait for the cavalry to ride in.

"And what is it exactly that I'm going to do to make the U.S. government go broke?"

"Simple. You are going to hack into the defense systems, as I've seen you do, and fire U.S. missiles on our petroleum, natural gas, and nuclear power facilities. You can leave the windmills. They please me."

Spencer delivered the final blow. "See, Digit? You get to spend the rest of your life working for the new government. It's a dream job."

Those words hit me hard. I checked my watch and saw that it was 7:55 a.m., almost time for my meeting with Professor Halsey. Was Bass standing around waiting for me to go to coffee, or did he know? Of course I'd been mad when I thought Spencer was trying to steal my boyfriend and lead me to slaughter and overthrow my government. But at that moment, knowing I was missing that job interview, it got personal. My flight instincts kicked back in, and the first thing I needed to know was where we were.

"What's the velocity of that river out there?"

Jonas seemed surprised that I'd taken an interest. "About four knots."

I laughed. "There's no way that river allows for that kind of flow. And there isn't even a large enough water body feeding into it. You must have some sort of regular energy source."

"We most certainly do not." I'd offended him. "Let me show you." He spread out a local map that showed the exact site of the compound. He identified the river and its tributaries.

"Oh, and at what point does the river pass by here?" I asked. He put his finger right on the map, in the exact spot of the compound, and I made a note of our latitude and longitude.

I nodded in understanding. "Wow. This place really is in the right spot." He was pleased with me. He'd converted so many people to his way of thinking that he probably expected my reaction. And I was his chosen squire, after all. I studied the map a little longer, though I had all the information I needed. Score: Jonas Furnis—a jillion, Digit—one.

"You are starting to understand. Our buildings impose on Mother Earth. We must build in response to her design, rather than try to alter her to accommodate ours."

I found myself nodding. Not that I was ready to become a card-carrying member of the Green Gangsta Brigade, but it was hard to argue with anything he was saying. Especially sitting in that beautiful setting.

"Are you ready to get to work?"

"I'm actually not thinking that clearly. Can we rest for a little bit first?"

Jonas was annoyed. "Fine. Throw the girl and the boy in the skirt into the room with the others. They have two hours. And our FBI agent, we don't need him interfering — take him out and make sure I never see him again."

EVERYONE SAYS I'M IN DENIAL,
BUT REALLY I'M NOT

AND SO BEGAN MAJOR MELTDOWN #1. I was aware that I couldn't hear my own scream. I was aware that I was being restrained and that if I strained my right arm any harder, my shoulder would dislocate. I was aware that I had been very wrong to be so relaxed. They dragged John out and he caught my eye. It was a replay of when they were going to kill us in that middle school in Brooklyn. That time I saw confidence in his eyes, encouragement. I didn't know it at the time, but he had a concealed weapon. This time I saw sadness or even a bit of an apology. He did not look like a guy with a plan.

Danny started to freak out. "Digit. They can't take him. Are they taking him? Digit, stop screaming." I still couldn't hear myself screaming.

We were led down a poorly constructed staircase into a damp basement. When the door to our cell was unlocked, I wasn't entirely surprised to see Adam Ranks slumped over on his bunk. I rushed over to him with that same suspension of reality that you have when you see a celebrity on the street. You feel like you know them so well that you want to run up and say hi, while they have no clue who you are. "Adam!"

"Mr. Bennett!" I heard Danny behind me, terror in his voice.

Mr. Bennett sat upright on the bunk directly across from Adam Ranks. This was the first time I'd ever not been happy to see him. I went over and hugged him anyway. I said, "They caught you. Now they have John."

He didn't have to say anything. I saw the pain on his face. He held me for a few minutes and let me cry. How awful, really, to be comforted by a man who'd probably just lost his son. But I was going to take anything I could get. After I don't know how long, I pulled myself together. A little. "Will they really kill him?"

"I don't know. He could escape if they don't kill him right away. But now no one knows where this place is but me. I should have called my wife." Danny was completely still. I couldn't even tell if he was breathing. Reality was sinking in. And reality's not exactly on my short list of favorite things anymore.

Adam spoke: "Is this the genius? Who's the kid in the hula skirt?"

"Oh, I'm Danny, Digit's brother. I would argue that you are the genius between the two of you. I mean, you create beauty, and now money, while she just keeps screwing up."

"Nice." *Jeez.* "Are you okay?"

"I am for now," Adam answered. "But they don't need me anymore. I turned over my technology so they wouldn't kill me. And now they're going to kill me anyway. Idiot."

"I love the evergreen. It's perfect." I was a little off topic and talking through a stream of tears, but I wasn't sure I was going to have another chance to say that to him.

"Thanks. That one's called *Natural Order.*" Of course.

"What are we going to do?" Danny was anxious to end the art appreciation lesson and get us back on track.

"I have no idea." Mr. Bennett said this while tugging on his ear to show that we were being listened to. He pointed to me. "I guess we're all going to have to cooperate. They actually do make a strong case against our way of life." He shook his head, unnecessarily, to show us he didn't mean it. He pulled me close and barely whispered, "Listen to me. John is a survivor. He's been trained to be. We work inside; he'll work outside. No more tears—we need to think. And we need you out of here. Deal?"

I barely spoke: "They caught you. And you've been trained."

"I'm old. I lost focus. John will not lose focus." I nodded, a lie to make Mr. Bennett feel better.

"I have no plan, that's for sure," I said out loud, nodding furiously to show that I actually did.

"I know. What plan could possibly get us out of this?" Danny was playing along now.

I wiggled my fingers as if at a keyboard, and smiled. "I have no idea."

I ALWAYS WANTED TO BE SOMEBODY, BUT NOW I REALIZE I SHOULD HAVE BEEN MORE SPECIFIC

I KNEW MY PARENTS WOULD BE FREAKING out by now. They hadn't heard from Danny or me since Saturday. My guess was that Tiki would have confirmed that no one had seen us and that my parents would have then contacted campus security and learned that it was all being handled by the FBI. Yep, they'd be freaking out for sure.

I had two seriously half-baked plans, neither of which I could safely run by my co-captives because we were under surveillance. All I could do was wait until I was called to action. And maybe enjoy the surveillance aspect of it a little bit. "How old do you think Spencer is? She looks kind of old when she smiles, you know, around her eyes."

No one was amused by me. Especially not Spencer, who swung open the door and announced, "That's it. Break over." Mr. Bennett squeezed my hand goodbye, and I followed her.

We walked down a long and poorly lit corridor that dead-ended into a set of wooden doors. Behind them was a state-of-the-art computer center with enough power to, well, take down the government for one thing. Computers and scanners covered one wall of the room, while the opposite wall was lined with neatly stacked twenty-dollar bills. A sole printer worked overtime spitting them out while one of the thugs made neat stacks of what was probably $10,000. It was a spectacularly simple operation.

The seat of honor was held out for me in front of three large PC screens. I sat down and stared at them. On top of the one on the far left was a small black box with its own alphabet keypad.

"We've wasted enough time, Squire." Jonas was a little anxious. "Show us what you've got."

A stomachache? "What exactly do you want me to do?"

"Get into the DOD." He must have seen my resistance-slash-horror-slash-nausea. "Or I'm going to slit your throat right in this chair. Got it?"

Loud and clear. I needed time and my laptop. "Let me see." I started looking through the operating system on his computer. With each keystroke, I was looking for a solution. If I didn't hack anything, he was just going to kill me. That I knew for sure. My only solution was to contact someone and let them know where I was. I needed my laptop.

"I'm sorry, sir, I'm not feeling it."

"You'd better start feeling it, or I'll have Wallace over there cut your feet off. We've done that before, and the stubs heal remarkably fast—you'd be surprised. But it sounds like it really hurts." *What the . . . ? Sweating here.*

"I told your, er, associate Spencer before. This thing that enables me to see the numbers and crack the codes, I have to slip into a sort of trance to do it. It's very strange, I know. But even just thinking about you cutting off my feet is shutting down my whole system. I need to be relaxed."

I saw it coming. Five, four, three, two, one. Jonas exploded. "Aaahhh! Do you think this is a spa weekend? I saw you do it. I watched you write the code myself. If I had known what you were doing, I would have recorded your keystrokes, and you would be decomposing in my compost heap already. You get yourself as damned relaxed as you need to be and do it." *Okaaaay.*

"I'm also used to working on my laptop. Your guys took it from me."

"Of course we did, but we found no hacking program on it. So whatever you've erased, you're going to have to reproduce. Now."

"Would it make any difference if I just did it on my laptop? I already understand my operating system, and I'm just more comfortable . . ."

"Fine. Just. Stop. Whining." He stormed out of the room and slammed the heavy wooden doors behind him. I started to consider what a powerful tool whining is, even more so than crying. Crying can appeal to someone who has an aversion to seeing you suffer, but whining is a whole different game. It's universally irritating. And in this case, lifesaving.

Wallace the Foot Chopper snickered in the corner. I had the strangest sense that he was staring at my feet and maybe estimating the diameter of my ankles. Jonas walked in a few minutes later with my laptop. "We've disabled your email, and I'll be watching your every keystroke. So don't try to do anything cute."

I flipped it open and got to work. I started building the most elementary hacking program, all written in C and completely convoluted. I asked Wallace the password to the wireless network so that I could try it out. He eyed me suspiciously. "Sir, how am I supposed to reach out and touch the U.S. government without access to the Internet?"

"Fine, the password is FurnisFire." *Ooooo, spooky.*

I decided to try my rudimentary program over and over again, attempting to gain access to various sites. My hope was that whoever had been monitoring my laptop for Mr. Bennett at the CIA was still doing so and would be able to locate us. After a while I remembered about the trance and moved my head from side to side with my eyes looking upward, Stevie Wonder style.

Wallace put his hands on my shoulders to steady me. "I'm

fine," I told him. "The code, it is being written through me." Now I was just messing with him. "We don't want to alert the government that someone is trying to get in until the program has proved successful. Let me try it on a less secure site, like a public university."

"Fine." His hands were still on my shoulders; no amount of shrugging was going to get him to release me.

Something was telling me that if I was going to get out of there alive, it would be my dad who'd save me. Thinking of John made me panic, and thinking of Mrs. Bennett made me feel guilty. But when I thought of my dad, I actually felt calm, like this was just one of our old challenges. I've been called childish, and thinking my dad was going to get me out of this might just prove it.

I easily hacked into the UCLA system, then into the Department of Mathematics and onto the platform that I knew would send automated messages to their central message board, careful to write only numbers. The first series of numbers I typed was my social security number, hoping that my dad would recognize it as me. Then I typed the first twelve digits in the Fibonacci sequence, hoping that it would remind my dad of the whole Jonas Furnis calamity. And then I typed 38.16, −81.19, desperately hoping he would recognize it as a latitude and longitude and come save me. It was a long shot, I know.

Finally, when I'd been online for over an hour and a half and was completely out of ideas, I knew I had to buy some time. I didn't want to get Jonas Furnis any closer to the DOD before we were found. I turned around and used my new weapon on Wallace. "I'm sooo tired," I whined. "I'm almost in, but I'm feeling dizzy and hungry, and I just can't concentrate. Can you just ask Mr. Furnis if I can take a break and start again in the morning?"

"You've got to be kidding. I'll let him deal with you himself." He left laughing and returned with a visibly agitated Jonas Furnis.

"Princess needs a little nap?"

"My whole mind is shutting down. I mean, I've written a lot of code and it works, but I'm so tired that I'm making mistakes. The past thirty minutes of work have actually been counterproductive. Please. Just let me clear my head."

"Fine. Throw her back in with the others. This is a joke." Another door slammed. I was beginning to like the sound of it.

HAS ANYONE SEEN WALDO? I'M STARTING TO WORRY ABOUT HIM

MR. BENNETT JUMPED AT ME WHEN I walked into our barracks. He put his hands on my face and looked me up and down to confirm that I was still whole. "Oh, thank God," he said as he pulled me to his chest. I was really no closer to being saved, but I somehow felt safe. When I pulled away, I saw the dark, worried circles under his eyes and under the eyes of everyone else in the room. Okay, maybe just Adam Ranks's. Danny seemed strangely fine.

"Dig, you okay?" Danny was kicking back on his bunk, a kid at summer camp between lunch and kayak races.

"I'm fine . . ." Mr. Bennett tugged feverishly on his ear to remind me that they were listening. "I'm just really so tired. I was stuck at first, but then they let me use my laptop, and I had a pretty easy time slipping into the trance and letting the codes reveal themselves." I winked at a smiling Mr. Bennett. "But I did all I could do for today. I'm beat. I just need to lie down." I whispered the rest into his ear. He smiled at the hope that someone at the CIA was still monitoring me, or that my dad would understand the numbers on his message board.

"Dinnertime!" Spencer burst into the room like a waitress on roller skates, fast and impossibly coordinated. She had a large tray of what looked like boiled chicken and a pitcher of water. No glasses. We all got up to eat, and Mr. Bennett sat close to Adam and whispered about what I'd done. Adam nodded and smiled as he listened.

Danny tore into the chicken like it wasn't disgusting. "Man, I'm starving. How long have we been here? Mr. B., what time is it?"

Mr. Bennett patted his watch sadly. "You know I haven't wound my watch since I was captured. I mean, what's the point?"

"Dude. Mr. B., get a grip. We're prisoners. They've taken everything from us, our freedom, fresh air. But they can't take away hope. It's all we've got. Now, you wind that watch and look toward the future, man. We're not dead yet."

Mr. Bennett actually started to laugh. "Okay, Danny. Here I go, winding my way into the future. Doesn't this kid make you miss California, Adam?"

Adam Ranks smiled sadly. "He makes me miss every-thing—my wife, my kids, feeling like I had choices to make. Though I guess I did have a choice to make here, and I agreed to do what they wanted . . ." Mr. Bennett waved his arms and tugged his ear. Adam went on, "Which was the right thing to do. Digit, you and I are a powerful team."

I knew he was just playing the whole pretend-we-are-on board-and-cooperating thing, but I started to feel the mag-nitude of the damage that could be done with our help. I longed to see the complete body of Adam's work and to know how much beauty he could create if he got out of here. And I thought of the meeting I'd missed with Professor Halsey, and all that I might have learned and contributed there. I just hoped to God that someone at the CIA was still stalking me. I had a lot I still wanted to do.

Spencer came in to collect our dinner things and take us each to the bathroom. It was a small room with a composting toilet. I don't totally understand what that means, but it has something to do with dehydrating our waste and reusing it? Let's move on.

"Big day tomorrow," she sang. Before she shut and locked the door, she turned back to me. "And, sweetie, we knew the CIA was monitoring your laptop, just like they knew we were. We took all that surveillance software off. They have no clue where you are, just so you know. Nighty-night!"

John and Dad were our last possible saviors.

The next morning we got to use the bathroom again. I'm just trying to think of the best parts of the day, and that was probably it. That, and the coffee. Jonas himself brought me a mug as I sat down to work. It even smelled better than normal coffee. He explained to me with pride how the water that they used was free of pollutants and that the organic soil was rich in nutrients. Everything you consume in harmony with nature tastes better. Apparently, he'd never had the chicken.

I went through six hours of the same old drill. I wrote code that made sense but that was so slow and cumbersome that it got in its own way. But all my keystrokes looked like progress to Wallace, who stood behind me and emitted an "Are we there yet?" sort of vibe. I finally asked to lie down for a few hours.

Back in the barracks, everyone was a little down. Mr. Bennett was lying on his bunk, silent and sullen. I sat down next to him and gave him a little nudge, saying, "Need Danny to give you another pep talk on hope?"

"No. One was plenty, thanks."

"You okay?"

He took my hand. "I miss my wife, that's all. And I'm concerned that I'll never see her again, that she'll never know what happened to us. And that she and I won't be able to spend the rest of our lives together like we said we would. Every day for a month, she asked me to move a stack of papers out of our bedroom in New York into my office. And I never did. I keep picturing her in our room now, looking at that stack of papers and remembering me as someone who didn't care to listen to her. And I should have. She's been telling me to leave you alone since I met you. That John deserved to have a relationship that had nothing to do with me. I've really screwed up. Not the relationship—you guys did that. But everything else. And John. I'm a little worried, I hate to say. If he'd gotten away, help would have come by now."

"I'm pretty sure you can just blame me for all of this. It's like one idiotic thing has snowballed into the actual end of the world. How does a nice girl with a nice 'gift' (*oh, yes, I did*) end up doing all this?" I was more sorry than I could ever admit out loud. "If I'd never cracked Jonas Furnis's stupid code, none of us would have ever met. We all would be fine."

"I'm not sorry about all of it. I'm glad John fell in love, even though it got off track. I just wish the two of you had a shot at forever. Margaret and I have been so disconnected lately. I've been distracted by my own project, this project really. And I didn't want to drag her into it because I knew she'd disapprove. But I couldn't let you fend for yourself out there, you know? There was so much for you to do, personally and professionally."

I remembered to whisper. "You think we're going to die in here, don't you?" The fog was starting to lift, and the obvious was revealed. Jonas Furnis was going to use my beloved jeans as insulation.

"Probably, Digit."

"If I have to do something really horrible, something that will allow Jonas Furnis to kill people, I'm not going to do it. Okay? No matter what. Are you okay with that?"

"Yes. And I'm proud of you. Your dad would be very proud of you."

This mention of my dad precipitated Major Meltdown #2. He had never pressured me and had given me so much room to grow into myself and my talents. He deserved more than to find me dead in a cave. And my mom, if she could see me and my dirty, snotty sweater, well, she'd probably die too.

I looked over at Danny and immediately looked away. Another life I'd ruined. "Hey, Digit, do you mind kind of getting it together? I have the weirdest feeling we are going to live through this, and that you're going to be sort of embarrassed about having acted like such a baby."

I wondered if it was a good thing that Danny was so clued out.

He went on: "The other night on the quad with those girls and this awesome skirt, I had a total epiphany about my life as a performer. It was so clear, like the future was revealed to me. Now, why in the world would I have had that totally life-changing moment if I was going to die in a few days? Why would I still be sitting here? In this skirt? Listen, guys, as long as you are with me, you're going to be fine. I have a purpose."

Adam spoke up. "He's impossible not to love. It's uncanny."

"No kidding."

WHO NEEDS TERRORISTS? WE'RE DESTROYING OURSELVES JUST FINE WITHOUT THEM

WHEN I GOT BACK INTO COMMAND CENTRAL the next morning, the mood had become more urgent. I knew the second I saw Jonas that he'd heard Danny's comments about definitely surviving and that they had irritated him. He turned my chair around and placed his chair directly facing me. Seated, we were knee to knee. I couldn't help thinking that this called for a table, a chess set, and a timer. For whatever reason, it was on.

Jonas said, "I'm running out of time." *Well, Zip-a-Dee-Doo-Dah!*

"Why's that?" *And, hello, why would you tell me that?*

"They're on their way." My shoulders relaxed and my forehead released; I thought I was going to cry again.

"Oh?"

"It's not time to celebrate, Digit. I've planned for this. And even before the game starts, I want you to understand that you can't beat me. I've thought of everything."

I wanted to start up an argument that Danny and I used to have when we were little, over just that expression. It's impossible to have thought of everything. *Have you thought of a frog dancing in his underwear through a desert? Have you thought of that lamp being the reincarnation of your grandmother?* We used to do this all the time.

He went on: "I want you to gain access to the DOD and arm

all available weapons to attack these coordinates." He handed me a sheet of loose-leaf paper with names of power plants across the country and their exact latitudes and longitudes.

"How does that help you again?"

"Energy production will halt, and this will bring the economy to its knees. We'll live in chaos for a bit, let the bodies go back to Mother Earth, and muddle through until we all just give in and embrace the prairie. I know you can do it, and I know you've been screwing around this whole time. I will give you two hours. Then I will kill you."

How far away were they? If they were twenty minutes away, I could just get to work. If they were three hours away, I'd be dead. I knew that I could hack the DOD in that amount of time. I could rebuild Oscar in half an hour. I also knew I couldn't cause that kind of damage.

"You're going to have to kill me."

"Oh, right. That. Like I said, I've thought of everything." His tone was overly casual, like he'd remembered to bring vanilla ice cream to serve with the apple pie. "Listen, I had a great computer programmer here. Wallace, when was it? July? Well, he set up all of my systems. And what I realized is that sometimes you can't force people to do things. A nuisance, that is. So he built me a little insurance before I killed him in case you were being difficult. Come."

He led me over to the three screens, the first of which had a small box on top of it containing ten digits and a timer set at six hours. I started to relax a little. If this was some sort of a code, I was back in my comfort zone.

Jonas started to laugh. "Sorry, but I have had the best time with this. It's perfect. This system, when armed, is set to activate my own stash of missiles that are pointed, right now, directly at Manhattan. It's amazing what a big box of cash can buy you on the black market. And the good news for you is that you get a little extra time. Once my system is armed, you have six hours to do as I ask or they will automatically fire. The detonator for those missiles is located in one of the power centers that I want you to blow up. If you blow them all up like I'm asking, the detonator will be gone and you'll have saved all the energy-sucking creatures in Manhattan. My guess is that you'll hack into the DOD to save the people." He watched as the impossible situation registered on my face. "Checkmate."

He was so smug, I wanted to punch him. "My recommendation is that you don't waste your time, or all those lives, trying to crack my password. You would have to live inside my mind to do that. Plus the password changes every five minutes."

What?!

And so began Major Meltdown #3. "What is wrong with you?! So many things that you say make so much sense and then . . ." I had to stop to wipe my eyes, again on that poor sweater. I turned to Wallace. "You know what? Get me a damn tissue!"

Reasonably mopped up and beyond angry, I went on. "Here you are, big Mr. I Heart Mother Earth, and you're going to bomb the entire city of New York? So you're the freakin' Guardian? I'm no expert, but I hear bombing's not that great for the environment. And even if I blow up all the power plants instead of Manhattan, people are going to die!"

"Aren't we killing ourselves anyway, my Squire? Isn't it just a matter of time? Mother Earth is going to attack sooner or later. Killing all those people is a timing difference. Tater Tots, young Digit—it's just like Tater Tots."

He gave me a second to really feel that comment. Then he went on, laughing: "Yes, I don't think there's a conversation that you've had in the past six months that I haven't been listening to. You might want to check your iPhone. And I have to say that your romance with the FBI kid was adorable. We've all been on the edge of our seats. Wallace and the others think you've been a little stubborn." He checked his watch and nodded to Wallace. "It's time for us to go. Sorry to miss the romantic reunion."

"He's coming?"

"From what I hear, he's bringing a crowd. We're out of here. I suggest you get to work. Manhattan blows whether I'm here or not." He reached behind me and typed something I wish I'd seen into the keypad on the black box. "And we're armed. Six hours, Digit." He turned to leave.

"Hang on a second. If you've got missiles now, why do you even need me? Why don't you just blow up the power plants yourself?"

"Ah, excellent question. Do you see how you were born for this work? The missiles I can purchase can target a multi-mile area like Manhattan, but they are not sophisticated enough to target a specific building. And from a sporting perspective, isn't it just a tad more fun to turn the government's super-smart weapons against them? Plus, spiritually speaking, it is your destiny to participate, my Squire. I couldn't have left you out."

"Seriously. You've got to stop calling me that . . ."

And he was gone. I heard lots of commotion upstairs—packing, I assumed. Doors slamming, and then silence.

Huh. If this was my destiny, wouldn't it feel good? I sat in that metal chair and started smoothing the invisible wrinkles on my jeans. The feel of the denim on my palms always soothed me. I tried to organize my mind. I had just received so much information, and I knew that if I didn't calm down, I couldn't process it all. John. On his way. I had to go tell Mr. Bennett.

I ran down the hall and burst into the room. "They're gone! John's coming! With a crowd!"

DEAR MATH, PLEASE GROW UP AND SOLVE YOUR OWN PROBLEMS

AFTER THE INITIAL WAVE OF RELIEF and euphoria made its way around the room, I explained to them my choice of either blowing up all the power plants or destroying Manhattan.

"The guy's off his rocker." *Thanks, Danny, no kidding.*

"There's a password that disarms the system, but it changes every five minutes. Last time I was there, the code read AGHDFEDD42. Even if I could crack it, by the time I was done it would change."

Again, Danny: "Sounds like it's Digit-proof."

"That was his plan all along." Adam seemed newly energized. He started pacing. "While I was building the printer, I heard him gloating about someone who could crack anything, but not if she was in a rush. The programmer, who's gone now, suggested they change the password every thirty seconds. But Jonas said five minutes made for a more sporting game."

"Digit, this is up to you." Mr. Bennett was firmly in charge, standing up to reveal his massive frame. "You have less than six hours. You can either spend it trying to blow up our nation's power sources, or you can spend it trying to find the password."

My choice was perfectly clear to me. If I went along with Jonas Furnis's plan, he won. If I tried to stop him, he'd probably win. And in my mind, his winning minus his probably winning equaled the possibility of his losing. That might have been an equation that only made sense to me, but I was going with it.

"First of all, let's get out of this room." I led them all into the computer room, and Danny and Mr. Bennett gawked over the ceiling-high piles of money. Adam slowly shook his head. The code read MNFDAYYA93. I grabbed a pad of paper and built a grid of the alphabet, with the corresponding numbers below it:

A B C D E F G H I J K L M N O P Q R S T U V W X Y Z
1 2 3 4 5 6 7 8 9 10 11 12 13 14 15 16 17 18 19 20 21 22 23 24 25 26

"Don't you want to use a spreadsheet?" Adam was over my shoulder, unimpressed with how slowly I was writing.

"She is the spreadsheet," Mr. Bennett told him. "Watch."

Jonas Furnis had used this kind of code before, so I thought I'd start there. It was strange that the eight letters would be followed by two numbers, almost like there were two parts to the code. I wondered if the letters were giving us a clue about the numbers or if it was the other way around. The ever-changing code was on the left-hand screen. Below it was the timer. I had five hours and fifteen minutes to figure out the logic, and then five minutes to apply it to shut this thing down.

With about four hours left, I was pretty much nowhere. I had a page full of numbers. That page and ten dollars could get me into the movies, without popcorn. In the distance, I heard a door open and footsteps overhead. I was so far into this impossible code that it barely registered with me. I actually was in a kind of trance.

"Digit!" I felt hands on my shoulders and a cheek on my cheek. I couldn't get up out of my chair. John got on his knees to look at me. "Are you okay?" He grabbed my face and kissed me.

"Sort of." I searched his face for a scar or a scratch, anything that was going to tell me what had happened to him. I realized something as I was saying it: "I never really thought you were dead."

John smiled and held my hands. "Good."

If my life story were made in Hollywood (close, next town over), this would have been a close camera moment. John and I would have filled the frame, with no room for extraneous information or people. If I were in charge, I would have kept the camera right where it was, but, in case you haven't noticed, I'm not exactly in charge. I felt the scene in the room expand to show other people, big well-dressed people who seemed to know Mr. Bennett. Some were taking notes on what he was saying; others were just looking around the room at the money and the equipment. And me.

Funny, I couldn't see through John's eyes how absolutely horrible I looked. But I sure saw it through theirs. I touched my matted hair and tried to push it away from my face. I rolled up my snotty sleeves. But just then, the invisible camera moved even farther back, and I saw in this scene something bigger than the people in it. The island of Manhattan.

I looked back at John. "Your dad can explain it all to you. I have less than four hours, and I need to get back to work."

Danny replaced John by my side. "Uh, Digit, one of the suits wants to know why we can't just unplug this thing. Kinda makes sense to me too."

I almost laughed. I mean, sometimes the simplest solution is the best. What if . . . ? What if I didn't have to figure this thing out, and I could leave and take a shower and a nap and get back to school and call Professor Halsey to explain. No such luck.

Adam knew the systems. "You can try, but I think it'll take more time than we have. There are no plugs around here, and everything is running on some sort of alternative energy source. If you can figure out how he hooks into geothermal energy and disconnect that, I have no doubt that the hydraulic system will kick in. If you can stop the river, he's still got the sun. He would never have left us with a simple plug."

I turned back to my work and was happy to hear the retreating footsteps of a few suits who were going to look for a sign that said PLUGS, THIS WAY! There were too many people in the room for me to concentrate.

Danny was not satisfied. "Why can't we take a bunch of guns and shoot at this thing till it doesn't work anymore?"

I perked up. "Can we do that?"

Adam shook his head. "We don't know if the missiles are idle and are waiting to be launched or have been programmed to launch already and are waiting for a signal to shut down. If we kill the system, we may have no way to stop them."

Great.

An hour later, I was beyond frazzled. I kept getting close to seeing something in the code, a second before it would change into a new one. Jonas was exactly right about the five minutes. I felt like if I had six minutes before the code changed, I could crack it. The numbers at the end of the letter stream varied between one and three digits, never higher than the number four hundred. Upon having that revelation, I thought, *So what?*

Behind me, the suits were chattering. "We made a full sweep of his office. A few files, some extra wires and stuff. Nothing on his desk but a bunch of maps."

"Nothing?" They weren't expecting me to speak. They looked at me as if they'd thought I was part of the computer. "There was nothing else on that desk? Not even a book? In the upper-right-hand corner?"

A few glances were exchanged. "No, nothing. Was something there before?"

"*Silent Spring.* Paperback. Green cover. It's not valuable. I mean, it's a weird thing to take with you when you are running for your life. Think of how much more money he could have carried on him if he'd left that book here." I was on to something. And they were looking at me like I was *on* something.

I thought of my dad. And *Go, Dog, Go!* No, I was not having my long overdue nervous breakdown. I just had a feeling that my dad and *Go, Dog, Go!* were going to help me. This may seem off topic here, but I absolutely hated kindergarten. Preschool had been fine, because I was fascinated by the new environment and all the kids in my class. But in kindergarten they were teaching us our numbers, like which numbers friends got together to add up to five. Let's just say I was bored out of my mind. So as a sort of bribe, my dad would place a coded message in my lunch box every day. It delighted me so much that I stopped complaining about school.

His codes were based off a single text— *Go, Dog, Go!* —which was my very favorite book. My favorite pages of my favorite book were pages 28 and 29, which are the most symmetrical pages in any picture book I have ever seen. The center of the Ferris wheel lies perfectly on the seam of the two pages, and even the words are balanced in either direction. Anyway, page 28 begins: "The dogs are all going around, and around, and around . . ." They just keep going around in this circle, no beginning and no end. This still relaxes me when I think about it. My dad always used the first lines of that page to encrypt his message.

So, let's say he gave me a cipher text like JCEDALLUGSJSTA. I would translate it into a series of numbers, based on their order in the alphabet: 10, 3, 5, 4, 1, 12, 12, 21, 7, 19, 10, 19, 20, 1, and then subtract it from the numbers that corresponded to my key stream, which in this case was only THEDOGSAREALLG because it was a short message. Here, that number stream is 20, 8, 5, 4, 15, 7, 19, 1, 18, 5, 1, 12, 12, 7. You just subtract them, so the first would be $10 - 20 = -10$. If the answer is negative or zero, you have to remember you are working off of a mod 26 clock and add back 26. So that first one would really be $10 - 20 + 26 = 16$. The second would be

$3 - 8 + 26 = 21$. The third is $5 - 5 + 26 = 26$. Keep doing this until you have a new stream of numbers, all 26 and lower, and then convert them to letters to get your message. So, 16 is P, and that's the first letter of your answer; 21 is U. (This message read PUZZLESTONIGHT and it was my favorite, because it promised lots of time with my dad and probably popcorn.)

I think we've established that I had an unusual childhood and an awesome dad. And do try this at home.

"John, get my laptop." John did as he was told. I wasn't thinking about it at the time, but it's really nice how he takes me seriously in these situations. Note to self: *Try to avoid these situations from now on and find other situations to be taken seriously in.* I stared at my page of numbers. "Go to Amazon. How many pages are in the paperback version of *Silent Spring*?"

"Okay . . . Rachel Carson, Houghton Mifflin, 1962 . . . here it is, four hundred. Why?"

Huh. Jonas Furnis was using a cipher text as his password. And I was guessing that it changed every five minutes to the first line of a different page of *Silent Spring*. That's what the number at the end of the code was all about. "Can you find a PDF of the book? It has to be the paperback edition, so I know where the pages begin and end exactly."

"Looking, looking . . . yes. Here it is. What page?"

I looked up at the code just as it was changing: RGFJH-PWOL170. "Page one seventy. Read me the first line on that page."

John read, "The presence of any pesticide . . ."

The countdown began.

IF YOU HAVE NOTHING TO DO, PLEASE DON'T DO IT HERE

I HAD TWENTY-FIVE MINUTES ON THE CLOCK, which meant that I had five tries to get this right. I had to take the letter part of the code on the box and convert it to numbers and then take the first nine letters on page 170 (THEPRESEN) and convert them to numbers. Then I had to subtract the *Silent Spring* stream from the coded stream to get a new set of numbers, which I would then convert back to letters and enter into the keypad. I started and was too late. I was getting so close that I was getting flustered.

The current code changed to HXVDQXLZB197. "John, read me the first line of page one ninety-seven. Hurry."

"And deceived the government chemists."

"*I* before *e,* or *e* before *i*?" This always baffles me, and if I was going to have to explain that question further, my head was going to implode.

"*E* before *i.*" So the nine letters were ANDDECEIV. Those letters translate into 1, 14, 4, 4, 5, 3, 5, 9, 22. The current code on the black box was HXVDQXLZB, which in numbers is 8, 24, 22, 4, 17, 24, 12, 26, 2. If I subtract that from the first stream of numbers, remembering to add back 26 when it's negative, I get 7, 10, 18, 26, 12, 21, 7, 17, 6. The answer is GJRZLUGQF, and I was thirty seconds too late to save Manhattan.

By this time John was completely onboard. The next code

was YDYEEUISJ48. John immediately got to page 48. "The first word is *predators*. It's nine letters. Go." And I started again. The room was completely silent, or at least it was to me. The camera angle in the movie version of my life was so tight on that piece of paper that there could have been an explosion in the room and I wouldn't have heard it. As soon as I had it, I typed ILTADATAQ into the keypad. Three beeps and a green light. Disarmed.

I sat back in my chair, with the adrenaline still raging through my body. I wasn't sure if I could move or cry or even regulate my breathing.

Mr. Bennett pulled me up out of my chair and hugged me. "You are an amazing girl. We've just got to get you working for the right people."

John was standing behind his dad, impatient.

"Mr. Bennett, if you don't mind, could I . . . ?" He let me go and I fell into John's arms.

Danny joined us. "Group hug! Not bad, Digit. Now I'm going for a walk. Anywhere." As he went upstairs, I heard him ask Adam, "Who gets all that cash?"

John led me out of the commotion, up the creepy staircase, through the now-ransacked first floor, and outside. I hadn't been outside in three days. The light stung my eyes and the cool air overwhelmed me. I took several deep breaths and took off my boots. I had to feel the dirt under my feet. I became aware of a loud noise above me and started to duck before I realized it was just the birds.

"I think I need to sit down." We sat at the base of a giant sycamore tree. The roots were spaced perfectly to fit us, like a love seat. John took my right hand between his two. "How'd you get away?"

"Knife in the sole of my shoe. Those guys are total rookies."

We both laughed, a little nervously. "So I'm starting to think maybe I need to get my act together." I turned to look at him and got a smile. "Tone it down a bit."

"Maybe if you need to get your teenage rebellion out of the way, you can just dye your hair pink or pierce something or smash people's mailboxes? Isn't that what they do on TV? I feel like the whole felony hacking thing isn't really working for you."

"It was stupid. And impulsive. Normal people just wait for stuff."

John started to say something and then shook his head.

"What?"

"It's just . . . I think that's what I was trying to tell you. I was upset and scared and so far in over my head in our relationship. I didn't say it right. I want to wait for you. I want to wait until we've got things figured out and can be in the same place, building a real life together. Not just having two lives that we're half living and trying to describe to each other."

"What if you meet someone else?"

"I won't. You might, but I won't. My dad would kill me." He smiled and put his arm around me.

"Am I going to go to jail?"

"We'll figure it out." Just then Danny walked outside, and the breeze caught his grass skirt and blew it straight up. We all laughed and the birds kept singing and the fresh air kept being fresh.

Don't you wish the story ended right here?

PUT ON YOUR BIG GIRL PANTIES
AND DEAL WITH IT

IN WHAT I NOW LIKE TO think of as my big Katniss moment, I realized when I got to Langley that a lot was going on while I was underground. My parents had moved into a Holiday Inn Express minutes from CIA headquarters. Mrs. Bennett had acted as their host, escorting them to the CIA every day and keeping them informed. When I arrived at Langley (uncuffed, thanks to Mr. Bennett), I found them waiting outside the director's office with Mrs. Bennett and my uncle Bob.

I rushed over to my dad, and Danny rushed to my mom. We switched. My mom was pleased to see that I'd showered. We had each had a turn in Jonas Furnis's rainwater shower, complete with homemade soap. I found several unused bars in his private chambers, each wrapped in burlap and seemingly uncontaminated by a lunatic's DNA. Assured that we were alive and smelled okay, my mom started: "Darling, your new sweater. Danny, where are your pants?"

Mr. and Mrs. Bennett were hugging and whispering to each other until John approached, the third wheel. Mrs. Bennett said how proud she was of him, and I could see that she meant it. She looked really tired and uncharacteristically un-put-together. I imagine that this is probably as close as she's ever come to losing her entire family. To my surprise, she came over and hugged me, a real hug. "Dear, I'm very happy that you are alive. No more trouble. We need you." I nodded, resisting the temptation to salute.

I turned to Uncle Bob, trying to hide my "What in the world are you doing here?" expression. "Um, hi, Uncle Bob. Nice to see you."

"Digit, I'm going to be representing you."

"I need a lawyer?"

"This is more serious than you may think. The CIA cannot and will not sweep this thing under the carpet. There has been too much media coverage, too much unrest on campus."

"Unrest? Why?" I hadn't thought about anything at all going on at MIT. I only knew the students on my hall, so I figured most people wouldn't even know I was gone.

"It started with a small group of hackers who see your arrest as a human rights violation. They think you've performed a service to the country by revealing a chink in its armor. Their enthusiasm has caught on, campus-wide. They're demonstrating for TV cameras; they're sleeping outside. That kind of unrest. The CIA is mortified, I think."

I turned to Mr. and Mrs. Bennett. "But the director, I mean, is it up to him? Isn't he your friend?" They were all staring at me, though slightly over my head. I turned around to see a very fit, very well-groomed man standing in the doorway to the office behind me. His face was so angular that I imagined his cheek slicing a tomato on an infomercial. With everyone behind me, he had to greet me first.

"Are you her?" He barked those words in a way that made me feel like he should have a clipboard in his hand and a whistle around his neck. The head coach of the CIA. *Go, team.*

I nodded.

"In my office. Now. Bring your lawyer." I took a step toward the office, and Uncle Bob, my parents, and John did the same. The director held up his hand. "You're an adult. Leave your parents, leave your boyfriend. Just bring your lawyer."

"He's not . . . we're . . ." I stopped myself from making a

distinction that didn't seem to matter here. *This guy is John's godfather? Are you kidding? Mine is my mom's cousin Jeffrey, who runs a summer camp and always has cookie crumbs in his pockets. Who'd pick this guy?* I glanced around to make sure I hadn't said it out loud. All clear.

When we were all seated, the director behind his desk and Uncle Bob and me in unusually low chairs across from him, the director spoke a single word: "Thoughtless."

Silence.

"Do you know what the word means?" Silence. "It means without thought. It does not mean that you were unable to think, which you most certainly are. It does not mean that you intended to do harm, which I have to assume you did not. It means that you acted without thought—without thought for the law, without thought for the consequences, without thought for your country. Thoughtless."

Silence.

Now usually when someone is thoughtless (and I now had a fairly clear understanding of the exact definition of the word), it's something like they forgot to write a thank-you note or they ate the last piece of cheesecake. These things can usually be fixed with a heartfelt apology. I gave it a whirl:

"Mr. Director, sir, I hope you can accept my apology. It was an impulsive thing to do, and I agree that it was thoughtless. I just wanted to get to a party because I had promised my roommate, who had a broken heart. And as you know, I was already granted access to the information, so it was kind of like a timing . . ."

"Please don't say 'timing difference.' You hacked into the DOD—this is not to be made light of. You will be charged with a whole bunch of things that the lawyers will come up with. In my mind, you are on trial for felony thoughtlessness. Your trial begins in two weeks." *Wait. What?*

"Trial? Is this a joke? I'm a college kid. I did something stupid."

"Again, you're technically a college adult. And, yes, you

did. Among other things, you have the right to a speedy trial. Now go."

You're probably wondering what I'm paying that cracker-jack attorney of mine. You know, the one who doesn't say a single word in my defense. I knew two things for sure: You get what you pay for, and it didn't matter at all. I had no case.

By four o'clock I'd been read my rights, formally arrested, and released to my parents on $40,000 bail. I couldn't tell by that number if I was a huge flight risk or a minor one. The CIA could move at warp speed if it wanted to, and they seemed to be in a huge rush to wrap this up.

Quick reality check: Sure, I was in a pretty stressful situation, but stress is completely relative. There is no absolute value to stress. There was a time when I thought that picking a lunch table was stressful. Of course, that was before I had to crack Jonas Furnis's asinine code to keep him from blowing up Disney World. So if you're wondering why I'm not curled up in a ball sobbing because there's a 99 percent chance I'm going to be thrown in jail for some period of my youth, it's because of these facts:

1. I am not dead.
2. Danny, Mr. Bennett, and Adam Ranks are not dead.
3. John is neither dead nor in love with stupid Spencer.
4. No one in Manhattan died yesterday who wasn't al-ready going to.
5. The U.S. government is still functioning.

At this point, a quiet year in a white-collar prison with time to think about all that had happened and what I was going to do with the mess I'd made of my life . . . Well, it didn't sound that terrible. And they don't even make prisoners wear stripes anymore (deal breaker). I double-checked.

WHAT A LONG, STRANGE TRIP IT'S BEEN

MR. AND MRS. BENNETT INSISTED THAT my parents check out of the Holiday Inn and that we all come spend the night at their house. I'm done saying, *What? You have a house here too?* I'm at the point where I pretty much assume that wherever they go, there's going to be a perfectly appointed home. This one was a normal-size house on a normal-looking street in McLean, Virginia. It had a welcoming porch with rockers and a freshly painted white swing with green-and-white-striped cushions on it. The front door opened to a wide staircase, with a living room on the left and a dining room on the right. Delicious smells came from the kitchen in the back of the house, and the fireplaces were lit. It smelled like normal.

Mrs. Bennett led us upstairs to the four bedrooms. Theirs, plus one for my parents, one for John and Uncle Bob, and a room for Danny and me. "Sorry, sis, you're bunking with me." Danny gave me a too-hard nudge and a too-big wink that made me wish the tiny landing was an awful lot bigger. And darker.

Mrs. Bennett saved me. "Danny, would you be averse to my offering you a proper pair of pants?"

"Averse?" He looked to me for a definition. "I don't think so."

After dinner I sat with my mom and Danny in the kitchen. We drank tea and talked about non-terror-related topics at home. Mom didn't seem too concerned that Danny had missed a bunch of school, and I waited for him to announce that he wasn't going to apply to college anyway. He didn't.

Instead he said, "Bet you never thought Digit would be the kid going to jail."

Mom looked up from her tea, eyes only. "At least she's dressed for it."

"Ha-ha. I'll be fine. Danny's new hula-girl look would probably get him the wrong kind of attention in there anyway."

"Hello, I'm wearing pants now. Brooks Brothers khakis, no less. How could you possibly get arrested in these pants?"

After tackling the big topics, I found John and Dad and Mr. Bennett on the front porch. They stopped talking when they saw me. "What's going on?" I asked.

"Just a couple of old guys meddling." Mr. Bennett gave me a little smile.

John put up his hands. "I found them like this. I've tried to switch topics, but my life is everyone's business now." He patted the seat on the swing next to him, inviting me to sit.

"It's not your life that we're all that interested in, son." Mr. Bennett gave John a nod and clapped his hands once. "So we're all clear here? Good," he said, and got up to leave.

Dad took his cue. "Yes, good talk. Good talk. Good night."

I maneuvered myself so that John would have no choice but to put his arm around me. Some people may not be familiar with this move, maybe because I made it up. It involves a bit of nudging in the direction of the person next to you. So much nudging in fact that the victim's arm feels a little short of breathing room. Invariably, the arm will rise up and rest around the assailant's shoulders. Disclaimer: I've only used this move on one person, but it works like a charm. "So, you guys have all the world's problems worked out?"

"Just ours."

"How's that?"

"We wait." Here we go. "Those two are more worried about you wasting your potential by hanging out with me than I am. It's not flattering."

I took his free hand. "So, I don't get to decide who I waste my time and potential with anymore?"

"Guess not."

"Come on. Be serious. What were you talking about?"

"I'm not sure if you're too close to see what's happened, or if you're too far away." He turned to face me. "We could have woken up this morning to a nation with no energy sources and a dead economy. We would have been subsisting off of a couple thousand windmills and whatever crops we could grow without tractors and farm equipment. Either that, or Manhattan would have been blown off the map. Do you understand what you did yesterday?"

"I cracked a code. It was a hard one, but it was just a code." I understood, but I wasn't comfortable pulling the camera angle back quite that far yet.

"You're smart, Digit. Lots of people are. But the government doesn't have anyone with abilities like yours. I doubt the world does. You're important to me, maybe everything to me. But yesterday you were everything to the world. See what I mean?" I really only processed "everything to me."

So I nodded, enthusiastically. "So what do we have to wait for exactly?"

"I don't know. But my dad is obsessed with my letting you be until you're twenty-three, and your dad is obsessed with all of us just letting you be."

"Twenty-three?" Don't make me do that math for you.

"I thought that was crazy too. I agreed to twenty-one. And believe me, I just want to take you to the airport right now and be gone. Like not check back in for twenty years. But your dad just asked me, what if you and I had been at the movies yesterday or hiking in Nepal? Jonas Furnis got all that money and those weapons without you. He could have just launched them, to get things going."

"So, you're saying if you and I are together, it'll be the end the world." I was getting the big picture here, but c'mon.

"Maybe."

This wasn't funny anymore. "So, really what's going on here is that you're breaking up with me because of my gift." *No air quotes, it is what it is.* "That's discrimination."

"Yeah, can we just get back to that? Breaking up? I'm not breaking up with you. I was trying to tell you that six weeks ago. Breaking up is what you do when you don't want to be with someone anymore. Trust me, Digit, I want to be with you. I want to take up all of your time. Can you hear the problem there? You are, at eighteen, a threat to national security and the key to solving any number of the world's problems. What if you had an education? What if you got to work with your precious Professor Halsey? Do you see? You can't miss that."

I did see. But what I couldn't explain to him is that I was exhausted, that maybe I didn't want to save the world. How did all these problems become my problem? And since when do all the world's problems cost you your boyfriend? I have honestly never heard of a person who has so many people trying to steer the direction of her life. "So what are you and the dads proposing again?"

"My dad is adamant that I not see you until you graduate. Your dad is adamant that this is none of his business. I think I like him as much as you do. But he is concerned about you missing out on your education. And toga parties."

"There was just the one."

John smiled and gave me a hug. "I'm glad you went. This is going to be worse for me than for you. You're going to be busy; I'm going to be waiting."

When did I get to be this high-drama crime fighter? I just wanted to go to college and see what was there, and suddenly everyone had all these plans for me. Even my dad, who tries to play it all neutral all the time. I knew he was silently cheering me into battle.

"Even that lunatic gave me choices."

"You always have a choice."

"Not between being with you and waiting. Or being normal and saving the world."

"You do. I just don't want to make that choice for you."

I imagined going back to school to work full-time for Professor Halsey and then coming back to my dorm or maybe a small apartment and having John there ready to take me to dinner or out for a walk to hear about my day. I let out a small laugh.

"What?"

"I think in my perfect world, you are my prisoner. That's not fair either, is it?"

"I think we've done enough of the prisoner thing. Here." John fixed the pillow at the end of the swing so that we could both put our heads on it and lie down. He kept his arm over me as we swung to keep me from falling off.

I had a thousand things to say, most of which sounded really good in my head. They were snappy movie script lines, the kind that would stay with him forever as he sorted through a box of old photos and remembered me as the one who got away. At some point, my mind must have rebelled. It had had enough of codes and puzzles, both numeric and emotional. My eyes were heavy, and I was relatively safe. I guess I dozed off in John's arms.

WHEN IN DOUBT, WALK THE DOG

☙

I WOKE UP ON THE PORCH SWING at seven A.M., and John was gone. Someone had covered me in a heavy down comforter and tucked it all around me. The morning was cold, but I could only feel it on my face. The neighborhood seemed to be awake and to have had at least one cup of coffee. There was a newspaper on the lawn, and in the distance I could hear a garage door opening.

I stared at the perfectly manicured hedge that defined the Bennetts' property. It wasn't the kind of thing you'd ever find in nature. Nature seems to work more in curves than it does in straight lines. Nature would construct a different kind of hedge; I guess it would be called a forest. I thought about the earth and the rivers over it, like my veins. I thought of Mother Earth as a living organism, being cut back and managed and tamed. All of a sudden my carefully tucked comforter felt like a straitjacket.

I freed my arms and found a small piece of paper on my pillow. "The waiting begins now. I love you."

By the time I went in for breakfast, I was puffy-eyed. Mr. Bennett informed me that John had left for New York at four a.m. No one had seen him go, so I couldn't ask about the puffiness of his eyes.

Everyone was seated in the kitchen except for the moms, who were scurrying around preparing way too much food. It seemed like one of those kitchen competition shows.

Danny was practically draped over his waffles. "What's wrong with you?" he asked.

"What do you think?" I was in no mood to play pleasant.

"Right. That."

Mr. Bennett and my dad looked at me intermittently over the newspapers. Mr. Bennett had folded the paper over so that the page facing me was a large photograph of Jonas Furnis and a headline: ECO-TERRORIST ESCAPES FEDS AND TEEN HACKER. The longer I sat there, the madder I got. I mean, I didn't volunteer for this. I really liked my boyfriend. I never even got to go to New York to do the whole romantic weekend thing. Or Hawaii, by the way! And now here they were, John included, deciding that I should be a monk and study my brains out so that I could help the stupid world with its stupid problems.

Mr. Bennett gave me one line: "Do we need to talk?"

"No. I get it. I don't like it, but I get it."

"Good."

My mom gestured with a wooden spoon. "Darling, have you thought of joining a sorority? I read that they rush in September, but you could start looking into it . . ."

"Rebecca, she's not a sorority girl." Mrs. Bennett seemed to think she was defending me, but her comment was my breaking point.

"Hey, how about this? How about since I'm old enough to be tried for a felony and sent to prison, how about we let me decide what kind of girl I am? And how I spend my time. Okay?" The kitchen was silent. I'd either gone too far or not far enough, I couldn't tell.

"I'm sorry, dear." Mrs. Bennett turned off the bacon and came to sit next to me. "None of this is fair to you."

"If I were just a normal person, I would be having a normal, happy life."

"If you were just a normal person, none of us would have ever met you." Mrs. Bennett put a hand on my shoulder, and I started to cry again. No one minded. Mr. Bennett went back to the paper.

Uncle Bob came downstairs with a healthy appetite for bacon and very little new information. (It also turned out that he was an entertainment attorney, dealing mostly with movie stars' contracts. You know, who gets their own trailer with a bowl of blue M&M'S, etc.) He informed me that I'd violated something called the Computer Fraud and Abuse Act.

"Is that all you've got?"

"Yes." He seemed to think it was plenty. "You got anything?"

"Sure. An ulcer and a future in an orange jumpsuit."

"No, I mean any ideas? You know, for your defense."

"The law's pretty black-and-white, and what I did was pretty illegal and intentional."

"Yes, there's that. I have some kids from MIT who want to speak at the trial in your defense. That's good, right?"

I imagined Tiki recounting the whole "Howard's a cheating jerk" story in gruesome detail. It made me feel better for a minute.

"And I think I remember seeing once in *USA Today* that in 2010 the longest sentence ever handed down for hacking was thirteen years. So we know what the worst case is. That's good, right?"

Yep, my lawyer was basing my defense on something he thinks he may have read in *USA Today*. That's good, right?

The next morning we said our goodbyes and headed up to Boston. Mom, Dad, Uncle Bob, and Danny had to get back to L.A. that afternoon and were, of course, coming back in two weeks for the trial.

Mr. Bennett gave me a long hug goodbye. "I'm going to keep working on this. I'm going to do everything I can to get them to cut a deal. And I'll be at the trial. Got it?"

Got it. I had a feeling I'd always have Mr. Bennett in my life, even if I didn't have John.

I went to half hug, half pat Mrs. Bennett goodbye and found my shoulders restrained by her hands. It was impossible not to look her in the eye. "Listen to me, dear. Your relationship with my son is not my business. My relationship with you is my business. You are a good girl. You are a smart girl. But you are just a girl. You need to get through this thing and claim your life. Don't let these men boss you around." *Jeez.* "If you need me, I want you to call me. Always."

"Thank you."

The CIA treated us to a police escort, ensuring that I would not be returning to school under anyone's radar. Two agents, who identified themselves as Phillips and Redmond, were dressed in MIT sweatshirts so they'd blend in when we got there. If "math majors who will not have a date until they're thirty" was the look they were going for, they nailed it. They drove separate black SUVs, one in front of our white rent-a-Chevy and one behind, making us look like a giant mobile Oreo.

The drive to Cambridge sounded a lot like this:

Mom: Darling, what part of "make good choices" didn't you understand?

Danny: So I had an epiphany when I was about to die in that lunatic's dungeon . . .

Me: I know, Mom, it was stupid.

Dad: Who are these kids that are testifying for Digit at the trial?

Uncle Bob: Just kids who volunteered.

Danny: Actually it was before that, on the quad at MIT.

Mom: That gorgeous sweater is ruined. I'm going to send you a few things as soon as I get back to L.A. Do you have a problem with corduroy? I forget.

Uncle Bob: They seemed nice enough via email.

Danny: So I'm not going to college.

Dad: Leave her alone, honey.

Uncle Bob: You think there's anything else I should be doing to prepare?

Danny: Just not yet. Maybe I'll try to get an agent and get some commercial work?

Mom: I've made an appointment for you to get your hair highlighted and your eyebrows waxed tomorrow. No arguments.

Danny: So I guess that's okay with you guys?

Mom: Honestly, darling. This whole thing could be televised. We'll need powder.

We all headed back to my dorm so that Danny could pick up his wallet and stuff. There had been no place to stash it in his grass skirt a lifetime ago when he'd left for the night. When we pulled up on the quad, I asked if we could sit in the car for a second so I could have time to prepare for reentry. I remembered the stress of being new here and dreading having to tell everyone my name is Digit and why. Again, it's so relative. Now that I have to walk in and tell everyone I'm back from being kidnapped and saving Manhattan but may be going away for a bit . . . explaining Digit seems like a walk in the park. A safe park, no kidnappers.

Phillips and Redmond went ahead to check the dorm. When they returned and delivered the all-clear nod, my dad hurried me out of the car. "Come on," he said. "We've got to get Danny's stuff and get to the airport. Let's go."

It was a beautiful afternoon, and the dorm was pretty much empty. We made our way to my room, and Danny quickly locked the door behind us.

A knock on the door made all of us jump. Danny motioned for me to get back, and looked through the keyhole. He whispered, "It's a guy, longish hair."

"Kinda handsome?"

"I guess."

A louder whisper came from the other side of the door. "Gee, thanks. It's Bass. Let me in."

Oh my God, I am so lame. Danny gave me a little smile and

waited for my nod to open the door. "Hi, I'm Danny, Digit's brother. And you are kinda handsome." Bass shook Danny's hand, and they laughed like they'd been buddies for years. People were just like that with Danny.

My parents and Uncle Bob introduced themselves. My dad joked, "They're always telling me I'm handsome too. I wouldn't take it too seriously." *Could someone please make this stop?*

"Hey." Bass took a step toward me but stayed by the door. "Welcome back. I'm pretty much up to speed, since you are on every local news channel and are the subject of every op-ed piece in the *Tech* . . . but are you okay?"

It was hard to know where to start. The answer to *How are you?* is always *Fine, thank you,* mainly because you know that whoever's asking doesn't really care. In this case, I felt like he really did care. His mouth was in a firm line, and his eyes looked a little pained.

"You want to take a walk?" Still I said nothing. "I need to walk Buddy anyway." I looked to my parents for help.

"Go ahead, sweetheart. We have to get going anyway. Danny, grab your stuff already."

Lots of hugs and *love yous*. As Danny left, he added, "Get some fresh air, while you can." Oh, he's just hilarious.

It took me a few minutes to find my sunglasses, which I desperately needed for protection from eye contact. We stopped at Bass's room to get Buddy, who seemed to remember me. A lot. Phillips and Redmond scrambled to keep up as we ran with Buddy across two lanes of traffic to the wide grass median that runs parallel to the Charles River. The trees were oaks and sycamores, different from the coral trees that run down the middle of San Vicente Boulevard at home. But the effect was similar, the feeling of a long, protected island between lanes of roaring traffic.

It was early November, and everything was orange and green. Some trees had gone completely orange, while others just had little hints of color at their tips. It reminded me of a punk hairstyle with a hint of pink at the ends. I knew that if I visited these trees the next day (and I would), the color would be creeping farther up their branches. *Mother Earth is a living organism.* And sometimes you can see her breathe.

I looked down at my blue jeans and green jacket and thought how perfect it was that I could walk through the fall without clashing with nature. Who knew that fall in New England would be the place where I was finally in step?

"So, you still have the dog?"

"I'll always have the dog. I've had him for two years."

"Then what was all that 'Hush-hush, keep-a-secret-while-I find-him-a-home' business?"

"Basic team building. Psych 101. I just wanted you guys to bond over thinking that you were sharing a secret. No one cares that I have Buddy here." He gave me a victorious sideways glance.

I smiled to myself. Not bad. Bass was enough taller than me that I had to take 1.3 steps to keep up with his every one. After a while I noticed that he was slowing down to my pace.

"So, you want to talk about it?"

"Which part? The part where I was fake kidnapped in high school? The part where the terrorists that were after me back then came after me again? The part where they're still out there? Or the part where I hacked into the stupid DOD so I wouldn't miss a toga party? There's also the part where my ex-boyfriend came back and saved the day and then sort of re-dumped me. Or that I'm on trial for a felony. Or that the government thinks I'm Wonder Woman now. Just spin the wheel and pick a subject. I've got no secrets anymore."

"We need to get you a better costume if you're going to be Wonder Woman."

"No chance."

"I had a feeling there was more to you than just the California girl with the nerdy nickname. You're very intense, but I didn't think it was because you were on the run."

The combination of the rhythm of our steps on the leaves, the hum of the traffic on either side of us, and our being side by side made for a natural conversation. With my eyes forward, I didn't have to figure out where to look. I don't know when I've ever had such an easy time talking to a relative stranger. It was like this on our last walk, and I wondered if we would ever be able to repeat these talks face to face. "I am intense. For sure. But I wasn't on the run from anything. I mean, I was trying to put that completely behind me. I thought I was going to be safe here. And normal. I think I'm more worried about missing out on having a normal college life than I am about going to jail."

"Were you hurt?" Buddy stopped to sniff the legs of a bench along the river. I looked out and marveled at how water can look cold. It's darker.

"Yeah. I don't really know what I expected. And sure I've probably made John look unprofessional with the FBI, but it seems like a bad time for him to be giving me my space or whatever. He's obsessed with this whole waiting thing, so that I can grow up and do whatever they think I'm supposed to do. Which I think is lame. I mean, if you're going to say you love somebody, can't you just figure out how to make it work? And just because I have this gift or whatever, does that mean I can't have a normal boyfriend to hang out with? It's like I have to pay for being smart by giving up my chance to be happy." Bass was laughing with his whole face, a rarity.

"What?"

"I meant were you actually hurt? By the terrorists. The ones who kidnapped you."

"Oh, nah. That was fine." We both laughed for what seemed like longer than the moment warranted. I saw myself as the poster child for mixed-up, lovesick teenagers-turned-adult (if there ever was going to be a poster for such a thing). And I felt totally okay with Bass knowing that.

Bass pulled Buddy along and we started walking again.

"He sounds more like your father than a boyfriend."

"Right? And the funny thing is that my father isn't like

that at all. I know what my dad wants for me, but he wants me to get there on my own time, if at all."

"I'm just happy that you're okay, at least physically okay. I was really worried about you."

"Thanks. But it would be good to be a person that no one was worried about for a change."

IF YOU'RE GOING THROUGH
HELL, KEEP GOING

↻

WHEN WE GOT BACK TO THE dorm, people were milling around the bike rack outside. It all looked pretty normal except something was off. It almost looked staged, but I couldn't quite see why at first.

Bass grabbed my arm as we approached. "Hey, are you ready for this? People have a lot of questions."

"I have a lot of answers." The only thing that kept this from being a total nightmare is that everything was out on the table. Everything about my first (fake) kidnapping had been unearthed in great detail. Even the fact that it was John who was protecting me then. I was pleading guilty to this new thing, and there were no facts that I had to remember to keep to myself. If my new college friends wanted to hear the ins and outs of my career in espionage, I could freely give them a complete data dump. In twenty-four hours we'd all be on the same page.

Clarke spotted us first, dropped her bike, and ran toward me. Over her flannel pajama bottoms and under her black leather jacket she wore a bright gray T-shirt that said FREE DIGIT in four-inch red letters. She threw her arms around me. "Oh my God." She shook my shoulders. "Oh my God." She hugged me again. "Oh my God. You're alive—you're standing right here. You're my hero, stickin' it to the Man. A trailblazer. Oh my God, in two weeks you'll be, like, a martyr."

"I'm not worthy. But I like your T-shirt."

"We've all got them. Even Scott's giving the black turtle-neck a rest. We had three thousand of them made, and everyone on campus is wearing them. There's a Free Digit Facebook group and #freedigit has been trending on Twitter for days." I looked around and saw it: Everyone was wearing that T-shirt. FREE DIGIT was everywhere.

I looked at Bass to see if this was a joke. He shrugged *I told you so* back to me and said, "Listen, everybody is pretty caught up in all this. If you want my advice, I say let's call a meeting in the common room and you can tell the story and answer questions all at once. Otherwise you're going to be repeating yourself for the next two weeks. We'll set a time limit."

I wanted to say: *I feel like you are the only person in the world who knows how I feel right now.* Instead I said, "Thank you," to his shoes.

I made it up to my room and had a text from Danny.

The T-shirts are classic. They let me bring ten home.

The big debriefing had to be moved from my dorm to the Engineering Department's auditorium because the crowd was going to be so big. I'll spare you the recap of the recap of the story of my recent life, but I pretty much started at the beginning with the code on the bottom of my TV screen back in the spring. I was relieved that people were a lot more interested in the way the cipher text code worked and how Jonas Furnis managed to run so much equipment completely off the grid than they were about my personal experiences underground.

And of course they wanted to know how I hacked into the DOD. I'd become a hero to the hacking community, simultaneously showing how flawed the system is and how smart hackers are. There was a lull in Digit-love when I failed to explain how I got into the DOD. It wasn't like I really blacked out when I did it, but maybe it wasn't such a good idea to offer a tutorial.

When the one-hour discussion was over, ninety minutes had passed. I was exhausted and hungry and a little overwhelmed. Tiki led me by the hand out the back door of the auditorium and leaned against the closed door as if to keep a wild mob from chasing us. "Those people are obsessed!"

We ran back to our room, laughing with relief, and ordered a pizza. Tiki caught me up on everything non-Digit-related that had been happening on campus. She'd changed her major and then changed it back again. Howard had been dumped by the brunette, and Tiki had sworn off beer and men — though she was interested in a guy in her studio art class who kind of reminded her of Howard. These sorts of problems washed over me like water in a warm bath. Normal people, normal problems.

At bedtime, when I went to set the alarm on my phone, I saw:

> John Bennett 8 Missed Calls. John Bennett 4 Voice Mail Messages. John Bennett 1 Text:
>
> I just need to know that you're okay.

I texted back:

> I'm fine. Wait. Am I allowed to call you?
>
> Why not?
>
> Waiting?
>
> We can talk when we need to.
>
> Must be fun to make all the rules.

My phone rang. "I know I seem a little obsessed, but you

always pick up your phone. I just wanted to know that you made it back."

"We had a big meeting here so I could debrief everyone about what's happened, mainly to save me the pain of telling the story a hundred times."

"That was a great idea."

"Yeah, Bass thought of it. People are a little over the top about this—I'm like the hacker's messiah. Plus now it's out about what happened in the spring and everything."

"The RA?"

"What?"

"Bass. Is that the RA I met when I was there?"

"Yes. So what happened at work?"

"It's hard to say. I was in meetings all day, answering a lot of questions. They reminded me repeatedly that I don't work for the CIA. They reminded me that it's not in my best interest to be the guy at the FBI with a convicted felon for a girlfriend. I told them that my personal life has no impact on my ability to perform as an agent. Not even I believe that. They reminded me that I left to go deal with my personal life in an FBI vehicle and did not return for a week. I sorta walked into that one." He laughed at the hopelessness of the whole thing.

"I'm sorry."

"Yeah, I know. Stop saying it."

"So am I going to see you before I go into lockdown?"

"Of course. I'm working on a couple of things that may take me to D.C. this week. But I'll be at the trial. Listen, the waiting is on, but I'm not completely out of your life."

DON'T RUB THE LAMP UNLESS
YOU'RE READY FOR THE GENIE

ᕲ

BESIDES THE FEELING OF IMPENDING DOOM, the next week was my best week at MIT yet. I was so happy to be back in class and even happier to have tons of work to make up. I felt like I was binging on my class work. The weather had turned colder, and people were wearing their FREE DIGIT T-shirts over their hoodies. It's crazy what you can get used to.

When I got back from class on Wednesday, Tiki hopped off her bed and pulled a huge flat box out of her closet. "This came for you. It's from California."

I opened the box to find a framed Adam Ranks print. There was no note, but the design was unmistakable. It was a large oak tree, deliberately symmetrical, with a 3-D overlay of a gold peace sign. It was the most tranquil piece of art I had ever seen. In the left corner it was signed *Adam Ranks 1/1*, meaning this was the first of a set of only one that would be printed. In the right corner was the title: *Peace for Digit*.

I just stared at it. I couldn't believe that it was mine, for me.

"We've got to hang it right now! I'm going to go see if your boyfriend has a hammer and a nail. Are we allowed to do that?"

"Call him my boyfriend? No."

"Put nails in the walls. And there is something up with you two. He never wants to walk that dog with me."

"That's because you don't care about nanoscience . . ." I called after her as she left.

We hung the print so that I was looking directly at it as I lay in bed. *Peace for Digit*. It was a long time coming.

But probably the high point of my week was on Thursday morning when Bass arranged for a redo of my missed meeting with Professor Halsey. The meeting was a five-minute walk from our dorm and was scheduled for eight a.m. At seven fifteen I was knocking on Bass's door. "Are you ready?"

"Are you kidding?" He opened the door in pajama bottoms and, well, that's all. Mercifully, Buddy leaped up at me and gave me someplace else to put my eyes.

"Yeah, it's a little early, but we should get going soon," I said to the dog. "I've been up awhile and thought maybe we could grab a little coffee first?"

"Fine. Could you maybe wait in the hall so I can get dressed?"

Buddy followed me out and we paced the hall together. Bass came out in jeans and a T-shirt that said DIG IT.

"Get it?"

"What?"

"I had my own made up. I'm all for solidarity, but I'm not exactly the kind of guy who wants to wear the same T-shirt as everyone else on campus." He walked down the hall to the bathroom, and I got it. *Dig it. Digit*.

Bass was still waking up when we sat down for coffee, and I started firing questions at him. "Is he still considering me for the job? Has he read anything I've sent him? Is he up to speed on everything that's happened? If he wants me, will he wait till I get out of jail, if I go to jail?"

He sat massaging his forehead as I spoke. "You are too intense for before eight o'clock."

"Sorry. How about you talk?"

"Okay, he knows everything that's happened. From the news and what I've told him. Like the whole administration, he's completely behind you. He wants you to return after you've . . . whatever you do. And he might hire you. He's worried you're a bit impulsive, a loose cannon."

"I get that a lot."

"So he just wants to get to know you. My advice — calm down." We sipped our coffee in silence. Bass looked up over his mug. "And it's hilarious what you've done with your hair."

"What?" I put my hand up to touch my freshly blown-out hair. I'd woken up with a little nervous energy; what else was I going to do?

"You didn't do that the night your boyfriend came to visit. But you did it for old Professor Halsey?"

"Again, I'm not normal."

My meeting with Halsey started with a bit of a scolding. It felt totally appropriate. The three of us sat around a small table in his office. A fire was lit in the corner, like he'd been there for hours.

"Miss Higgins, may I remind you what nanoscience is all about? We strive to alter something at the smallest level to create change in a larger organism, structure, or process. You are one person, maybe not even a hundred and ten pounds, and every minute you are faced with choices that shape the larger structure of your character and your life. Everyone does. But for you, with your abilities, the choices that you make for yourself are going to impact the larger organism more quickly than mine or Sebastian's or anyone's. I need to know that you fully appreciate that."

"I do."

"You were used as a weapon. If I hire you, after your incarceration, you will have to be more prudent in your decision making."

"*If* she's incarcerated, sir. We still have a trial to get through."

"Son, she's going to jail. She broke the law and humiliated the Defense Department. This has turned into the United States versus the students of this university. The government will win. But when you are released, I will hire you. Sebastian can take you through some of our current research before then if you'd like, and you can start in earnest upon your return." He stood up to indicate that we were done and added, "And the pay's terrible. Be warned."

"That's why I have four other jobs, sir," Bass said as he led me out into the cool morning. I buttoned up my jacket and strapped on my backpack and turned to look back into the office where Halsey was sitting at his desk.

I gave Bass a little shove and then a really big hug. "Can you believe this?! I'm hired! I mean, after jail or whatever, but I'm hired. By him."

Bass was smiling, eyes mostly. "Congratulations."

"When can we start? He said you could tell me stuff. Can you? When? Do you have class right now?"

"I need to walk Buddy. Come with me." We went back to the dorm to get Buddy and warmer jackets. Phillips and Redmond trailed us as we walked for about a half an hour and then tried to look inconspicuous when we stopped to sit and look at the Charles River for an hour. Buddy ran around with the other dogs, and I learned a thing or two about the practical applications of nanotechnology. Namely (are you sitting down?): Scientists are using silver nanoclusters as catalysts to reduce the pollution generated from manufacturing plastics, paint, and detergents. Nanowires are being developed for use in solar panels that generate more electricity at a lower cost. They're making an epoxy that contains carbon nanotubes to make stronger and lighter windmill blades. There are iron nanoparticles that can clean up pollution in our groundwater. And, hello, there's a nanotechnology that lets scientists capture carbon dioxide in the exhaust stacks of power plants before it's released into the air.

"I feel like I'm going to pass out."

"Yeah. It's very cool."

"But does everything you're working on have to do with the environment? I never knew that he specialized like that."

"No, he works on lots of different applications. Some of that isn't even our research. I just thought you'd be interested in that part since, well, what you just went through. And your interest in trees."

"Thanks." We stared at the water for a while. I loved being in a place where my mind was occupied enough so that I didn't have to babble. "You know what's kind of sad? There's one person I'd like to be able to talk to about all this."

"The boyfriend?"

"Jonas Furnis."

"Really?"

"Yeah. Half of what he says makes so much sense that you almost want to run off and join his merry band of thugs. He crosses the line into murderous violence because he's crazy but also because he thinks it's all so hopeless. I wonder what he'd think if he knew there was this kind of hope."

"Maybe that's your next step. Getting it out there."

"That's what I've always dreamed of doing. Taking the stuff that's in my head and then applying it to real problems and delivering it to the world in a way that helps. It seems so simple. Like I've always imagined a conversation with the president about all this. And this was even before I got here and before I understood what a difference science can make to our survival. Like the butterflies. The president should know about the butterflies made of tiny solar panels on Jonas Furnis's roof. They were beautiful—people would pay for that. There should be an infestation of butterflies on top of the White House. People should know about this stuff, not just hippies and activists. It should start at the top." I became immediately aware of the urgent pitch of my voice. It sounded like begging, and I knew I'd gone too deep. People don't need to hear about your wildest dreams. I'm sure Bass was waiting for me to tell him I also wanted to be a ballerina. "Or not. I mean, it would just be cool to talk to the president."

"I bet you ten bucks that conversation is going to happen."

"I'll take your ten bucks. I'm just not up for going after it anymore. You know how after an adrenaline rush, you just get kind of sleepy? I've been on an adrenaline rush for half a year. I'm really sleepy. Maybe that's why I like it here so much: I can read and think, but I don't have to be part of the bigger world."

"I get that. You deserve to hunker down a little. But eventually you are going to have to move your ideas out into the world. And meet people with influence to make change happen. Professor Halsey can't change the world from behind his desk. We're going to have to get out there. At least I am."

That sort of felt like a dare. "Don't make me feel bad if I decide not to be Wonder Woman. I can be a perfectly productive member of society staying right on this campus forever, thinking about stuff. I'll get a dog to walk."

"Sure. If that's what you want to do. But don't think there's something noble about it. Being small doesn't make more room for other people."

"You're smart."

"Everyone here is, remember? And at some point you have to decide if you're a thinker or a doer, or both."

"What do you mean?"

"Like running . . . you can think about running, you can read about it, but . . ."

"I'm not a runner. New example, please."

"Okay, kissing."

"Haven't been doing much of that lately either."

"Let's say I wanted to kiss you right now."

My hands flew up to protect my face. I was suddenly so embarrassed, and that crazy red heat was all over my cheeks.

"I'm not going to. Would you get over yourself, Digit?"

"Okay. Sorry." I replaced my hands in my pockets where they belonged.

"I could think about kissing you all day. I could even talk about it with my friends and watch great first kisses in a hundred movies. But at some point I'm going to have to just bust out and do it. That's using a totally different part of yourself."

"Your lips?"

"Your courage."

We walked back to the dorm in complete silence. I was starting to see the possibility of me coming out of college as two different people: one who read research and maybe wrote research and had a normal boyfriend who liked to share popcorn at the movies on Friday nights, and one who used what she had and what she'd learned to create something.

When we got back to the dorm, he asked me, "Walk tomorrow?"

"Sure. Seven fifteen? We can bring our coffee."

"Just let me sleep till eight. I'll come get you."

TAKE MY ADVICE — I'M NOT USING IT

THE NEXT TEN DAYS PASSED IN much the same way. I caught up with my schoolwork and became an avid dog walker. Even in the rain. (Who knew you still have to walk a dog when it rains?) The leaves covered the park and made the pathways slippery as we walked. Once a week they were blown into huge piles by crews of maintenance guys. By the next day, the wind had scattered them back around, where they were meant to be. *Mother Earth is a living organism,* I thought. *And she'll have her own way.*

I usually came away from these walks with more questions than answers, so Halsey let me stop by in the afternoons to talk. He seemed to understand that I was a person who needed to be contained, so he set a timer for fifteen minutes every time I set foot in his office.

On the Saturday before the Monday when my trial was scheduled to begin, Bass and I were on our regular nano-walk.

"You scared?"

"I've seen worse."

"I bet. Maybe we should get everybody together and go out for dinner tonight. Like to celebrate? That's probably not the right word."

"Everybody?"

"Just Tiki and the hackers." It was starting to sound like a garage band. "There's a pretty good bistro in town. They said they'd give us the booth in the corner that they usually reserve for people having political meetings or affairs."

"How do you even know that? Are you into politics or old ladies?"

"I work there on Thursday nights."

"Honestly, how many jobs do you have?" I was trying to remember all of them: RA, research assistant, band member, now waiter?

"Four, sometimes five. What? College is expensive. Haven't you noticed?"

Truthfully, I hadn't. It hadn't even been a point of discussion for my family when I was looking at schools. There was a silent assurance that anywhere I wanted to go would be fine. My parents pay the bills, I'm on a food plan that covers all my meals, and I get a small monthly allowance. Not only had I not noticed it was expensive — it all seemed free.

I realized that I had become the worst kind of self-centered person. Everything was all about me, even down to the T-shirts. And I didn't know anything about Bass. Not where he was from, nothing about his family, not even where he got that dog. It seemed almost too late to ask. All I could tell you about him is that he's really smart, can smile without moving more than six facial muscles, and tends to express himself through his T-shirts. And he knew plenty about me.

Everyone was excited about our "celebration" dinner. I wore the new replacement sweater my mom had sent and blew out my hair. Tiki gave me a whistle. "Well, look at you, with smooth hair and slightly different clothing. Is this just for us?"

"It's sad that a minimal amount of primping seems like an occasion." My mom had also sent a navy blue dress for me to wear to the trial. It had absolutely no pattern and had pockets to hide my hands in if I got nervous. She's thoughtful like that. The trial couldn't last more than a few days, and she probably knew I would have no problem repeating the outfit.

We all met in the hallway to walk to dinner. Bass nodded at my hair and said, "Interesting."

Tiki agreed. "Right?"

"Can we just go?" I begged.

The restaurant was dark and loud and festive. Bass was greeted with a hug by the beautiful French hostess and then got a kiss on both cheeks. Was this really necessary? You could walk away pregnant after a greeting like that. The rest of us got curt nods as we were taken to the mysterious corner booth.

We shared mussels, roasted chicken, and Caesar salads. The waitress brought us appetizers that we did not order, with a wink to Bass. He thanked her warmly, and she stayed too long, waiting for more. I watched him talk with Clarke, nodding in approval but interjecting when her theories were getting too outlandish. He was never too light or too serious. He was a person in balance, like Danny with focus.

"Star-ing!" Ella nudged me a little too hard in the ribs. "Digit, this is getting so embarrassing."

"Totally. I've been watching it too." Scott was shoveling salad into his mouth but didn't miss a beat. *Why isn't anyone whispering? This seems like an occasion for hushed tones.*

I don't know how I knew, but I knew Bass heard. Something shifted in his jaw and in his shoulders when Ella said it. I guess I knew because I was still staring.

We walked back from dinner, all laughs. Everyone was full and relaxed. The dorm was at a medium to low level of activity, but kids studying in the common room barely looked up when we walked through. Bass had been right about the one-shot intensive info session—it had gotten me out of everyone's system. Clarke, Ella, and Scott turned into Scott's room. "We're going to work on our science project. Night." Winks all around. I'm still not sure why Clementine had to be such a secret. I suspect the secrecy was part of this carefully cultivated hacker lifestyle (complete with fake glasses).

We got to our end of the hall and stopped at my door. From a thousand miles away it would have looked like an end-of-date moment. Except that Tiki was standing there too. I searched my bag for my keys, and Bass stood waiting with his hands in his pockets. Tiki grabbed the keys from me and went inside and closed the door without saying a word, making it feel like an end-of-date moment. I'd stood here talking to him every day, finishing up our conversations about oil spills or whatever. But this was different—darn that hair dryer.

I looked up at him and then quickly away before I said, "Can I just ask you . . . um, where are you from? Do you have siblings, and where'd you get Buddy?"

Having gotten my questions out, I searched for a new spot to put my eyes. They settled on his left hand, which was rising out of his pocket, on track to come up and make contact with my face. My face went hot in anticipation. I'd just tell him I suddenly had a fever. Doesn't that happen to people? They go out, they have a lovely time, and then *bam!* they're hit with the bubonic plague or food poisoning?

His hand paused at eye level and counted off one, two, three as he spoke. "Canada. Four. The pound."

"I didn't know anything about you."

"There's not that much to know. No one's chasing me." *Yeah, except all the women who work in that restaurant.*

"Count your blessings," I said, like I was someone's grandmother now. Next time I'd be sure to leave him with "A stitch in time saves nine."

He didn't seem to be making any move to leave. Neither did I. "You have a hard time looking directly at me."

I looked directly at him, just to prove him wrong. "See?" And then I immediately knew why I never looked directly at him. His eyes were stronger than mine, probably from doing all the work for the rest of his face all these years. I was locked in and feeling dizzy and oddly aware of my mouth. I bit down on my lip to ensure it was still closed.

And then my phone rang. I reached into my pocket and answered it, still unable to move my eyes. "Hello?"

"Hey. What are you doing?"

Bass's eyes smiled when he heard it was John.

"Waiting?" I bit down harder on my lip.

"For me?"

"Sorta."

Bass leaned down and kissed me at the intersection of my cheek and the corner of my mouth, saying, too close to the phone, "Good night, Digit."

"Is that the RA?"

Bass turned to walk back down the hall. The spell was broken, and I could move my eyes anywhere I wanted, but my stomach was still doing flips.

"Digit? What's going on?"

I slumped down on the floor in the hallway and tried to get it together. "Hey, nothing. We all, a bunch of us, just went out for dinner. You know, a last hurrah before the slammer. But everyone's gone now, perfect timing."

"This is torture."

"Yeah. Tell me about it." I watched as Bass closed the door to his room. "You in New York?"

"I'm back in D.C. I just wanted to make sure you were okay. I'll be up there Monday morning."

When I hung up the phone, I sat for a while. The hallway was no longer threatening in any way. It felt like home, and I was happy to sit there all night, in that in-between space. That is, until the door to Bass's room opened.

I started to get up, maybe to take flight or maybe to run over there—I guess I was just going to let my boots decide when the time came. Bass walked out with Buddy on a leash behind him and, instead of walking toward me, just gave a quick wave and turned the other way to take the back stairs out. He doesn't take the back stairs at night. No one does. The back door is always locked at this time of night, so he was going to have to go downstairs and then cross back to the front of the building to get out. That was maybe fifty extra steps just to avoid talking to me.

As part of my new effort not to be so totally self-involved, I tried to put myself in his situation. What if I just tried to kiss someone, although at the absolute wrong moment, while they were on the phone with their old girlfriend who they were totally still hung up on? As hard as I tried, I just could not put myself in that situation. I couldn't imagine kissing someone without a written invitation. It was a different sort of psyche. Sure, I'd think about it. News flash: I'm an overthinker. But unless it was a life-or-death situation, I wasn't sure I had the courage to be a doer at all.

I managed to get into my room and shut the door completely before Tiki could start *Ooooh, girl*-ing me. "Stop."

She was lying on her bed, smiling like she'd just heard a juicy secret. "Okay, fine. But there's something up . . ."

"No. Nothing's up. We're friends. We have things in common—okay, everything in common. But that's it. Trust me, no one's hot for the jailbird."

SOME DAYS YOU'RE THE WINDSHIELD; OTHER DAYS YOU'RE THE BUG

ᘓ

SUNDAY STARTED OUT NORMALLY ENOUGH. TIKI and I were in our room studying. Some might think this was a little unnecessary, since I was not likely to be in class for the rest of the semester. If they lived inside my head, though, they would know it was more than necessary. Unfortunately or fortunately (it's hard to tell which—there's a fine line there too, as it turns out), the hackers stopped by to show us the final programming changes to Clementine before the big robot fair.

Everyone knew about Clementine but Bass. They'd mentioned their (*wink, wink*) science experiment about a hundred times in front of him, but either he was not interested or he was just playing along with the whole mystery thing. He never asked for any more information.

Scott was so excited that I started to get excited for him. He placed Clementine on the floor with a big paper bag next to her.

"I don't have all day." Tiki was not particularly interested in spending the day inside playing with a robot.

Scott said, "Wait. Let's show Bass. He won't tell anyone. We haven't said anything about the dog, right?"

"He doesn't need to see it. Come on, Scott, go ahead." Now I wanted to get this moving as much as Tiki did.

"He's right. Go get him, Digit." *Why me?*

"Clarke, you can go get him if it's so important." Everyone looked at me to see why I was being so difficult. It would take me twelve seconds to walk down the hall, knock on his door, and get him. "Fine." It actually took me closer to thirty seconds to get to his door. And another thirty to knock on it.

"Hi."

"Hi."

"Need something?"

No words came out. Luckily for me, because the ones I had racing around in my head were not to be repeated. Even here.

"I was just going to take Buddy out. Wanna come?" That sounded so normal. Maybe I'd just overreacted to the little demi-kiss. Maybe we could just go back to walking the dog and talking science and funny T-shirts.

"Sure. But can you come down to my room for a sec first? Scott has something he's dying to show you. It's cool, I promise."

"Sure." See? Everything was totally normal.

Scott insisted we close the door before he started. "Now, Bass, you are sworn to secrecy."

"Me and everyone else on the hall—now get started or Buddy's going to pee all over my room."

Scott placed Clementine on the floor next to the paper bag and pressed Go. Clementine released her little penguin arms, emptied the paper bag, and stacked its contents (ten Coke cans) into a perfect pyramid. Then she backed up and shot them down. We all cheered, because we were expected to. And because it was awesome.

Ella took the cans and put them back in the bag so we could see it again, and we all stayed in my room to watch. This was unfortunate because about five minutes later Jonas Furnis walked in and locked the door behind him.

POO POO OCCURS

EVERYONE LOOKED UP, WITHOUT FEAR, BECAUSE they had no idea who he was. "Hello, Squire." He was in a brown trench coat and a black skullcap, which protected his baldness from the Massachusetts chill.

Bass got up and started to say something, but Jonas pulled a gun out of his pocket and told him to sit. "I will kill all of you. That's not a threat—it's why I came. I'll do it fast now or fast a little later. It makes absolutely no difference to me."

I suddenly missed my buddies Phillips and Redmond. "How'd you get in here?" I asked.

"I detonated a small cache of fireworks at the back of the building. They went to investigate and I walked right in. Digit none of these people you trust are your intellectual peers. They're imbeciles."

"We need to talk. And I'll get you out of here." I tried to sound calm. "There's a lot that you should know, amazing things. But these people have nothing to do with you or what you're doing. Let them go. And we can talk . . ."

"Digit, I've had plenty of time to talk to you. Do you really think you have any light to shed on any topic that would be of interest to me?" *Yes*. "You have shown me that you are a worthy opponent. And I see now that you are not going to cross over to Mother Earth's side. As her Guardian, I declare you her enemy. The punishment for a disloyal squire is death."

Clarke looked like she was going to cry. Scott looked worse. I was scared, of course, but also a little confused. This didn't seem like his style, just walking in here and killing me. Where was the sport in that?

"First things first. May I have all of your laptops and cell phones in a pile right here?"

We had two laptops and six cell phones between us. Jonas seemed satisfied but Scott blurted out, "No, I have another one!" and handed him his Blackberry.

"You've got to be kidding me." Clarke smacked him in the arm. Scott covered his face.

Bass was slowly inching closer to me. For what, I don't know. Unless he'd popped in for the Sunday morning science experiment packing heat, he was useless to me.

"Thank you, young idiot. Now this is very simple. No one leaves this room but me. Today is not my day to die. I have a spectacular explosive planted in this building that will flatten it completely in a matter of seconds. It's set for one hour from now: You will be in nano-pieces and I can go on with my life."

He walked over to me and kissed me on the top of the head. The creepiest part is that he seemed to mean this. "You are the last person I wanted to have to kill. I truly believed that you'd been sent to help me. My disappointment is profound."

Both of Adam Ranks's posters caught his eye. "Ah. I see you're a collector. This one's new. Pretty. Yes, now these will be destroyed as well in an hour, and then I'm off to California to finish the job with Mr. Ranks. We were sloppy letting him outlive his usefulness, weren't we?"

Bass had now maneuvered his body between Jonas's and mine, which was a nice gesture, but it's hard to stand between someone and a bomb.

Jonas approached the windows. "Breathtaking day." He attached a small device to the latch of each. There was a split second where his back was to us, but none of us had the presence of mind to jump him. We all just sat.

"Now, trust me, no touching the windows or the door.

You'll be greeted with a most unpleasant kaboom." He turned to leave.

"Jonas!" I shouted.

"Yes."

"Where's the fun? I don't even get to crack a password or anything?"

"The timer's already running on the bomb and on these devices. Only I know the password to disarm it. There's no code to crack, just a password. But even if you thought you could guess it, you're stuck in here and I have your phones. You're right, it's not very sporting, but I've had a rough few weeks. Sometimes you just need a quick victory." He placed another small device on the doorknob before he left, saying, "Checkmate."

Clarke took the opportunity to smack Scott in the head. Ella sat down and started to cry. Tiki paced. Bass put his arm around me. "We're not going to die in here. If I can stay calm, can you?" He took my hands. "Seriously, let's think. We have an hour. We need to communicate. We need to clear everyone out of this building. We need a phone." Everyone looked at poor Scott again.

"Sorry!"

Ella suggested we tape a sign to the window, but I was scared that even the tape touching it would blow us up. I had no idea how sensitive Jonas's explosives were.

"What if we try to wave someone down, just to let them know there's trouble?" Bass walked to the window just as four police cars pulled up in front of the dorm. "The cops are here. How could they know . . . ?"

I stood next to him in time to see Jonas Furnis crossing the quad, with his coat flowing behind him. He stopped and raised his arms like a bird. For a second I thought he was going to take off, the Guardian taking flight and leaving Mother Earth. I was half right. A shot had been fired, and with raised arms he fell forward.

"He's dead. They must have been following him."

"Thank God," the hackers said. I felt no relief as I said it.

"Except he was the only person alive who knew how to disarm the bomb that's going to kill us in fifty-five minutes."

"Let's take this in pieces." Bass was speaking only to me. "Our first responsibility is to get a message out to clear the dorm."

Ella started shouting at the door, "Anyone out there? Don't touch this door, but can you hear me?" We were pretty much half the hall, and everyone else was probably out or still asleep.

Scott collapsed on Tiki's bed, cradling Clementine in his arms and whispering to her. "It's okay, don't be scared. I'm not going to let that bad man's bombs turn you into nano-pieces."

Ella put her head in her hands. "All that work. All those tiny little screws. Everywhere. What a waste."

Clarke chimed in, "You're a total waste. You even used my old Droid . . ." They all looked at each other and then at Clementine. "Rip her apart, Scott. Or I'll do it myself."

Apparently, Scott had used an old Android phone to work as Clementine's communication system. He painstakingly opened her up and pulled it out. "It's still charged. Three bars."

"Dial 911. Or no? Digit, who should we call?" Bass seemed to think I was the authority on these situations. And, looking around, I guess I was.

"Let's call 911 first." I dialed and explained in as simple terms as I could what our situation was. I asked to be transferred to one of the police officers outside in the quad. They were putting police tape up around where Jonas Furnis's body still lay.

I got one of them immediately. "This is Digit Higgins. I'm in McKinsey dorm at MIT. Yes. Free Digit, that one. Yes. I can see the body from my room. That's the guy. There's a bomb in this building and it needs to be evacuated. Is there a bomb squad nearby? We don't have time for that. I'm in my room with five friends, and the windows and door are booby-trapped. We can't get out unless that bomb is disarmed. We need . . ."

Bass took the phone from me. "This is the RA. Please evacuate this building. Then go to room 205. You will find a dog named Buddy there. He is reasonably friendly, yes. Walk him up and down the halls. He'll find the bomb. We only have forty minutes left."

Within five minutes, the building was surrounded by police cars. Dozens of cars filled with dozens of cops, none of whom knew the code to disarm the bomb. Even if Buddy found it, it couldn't be dismantled without the code.

Sounds of barking made their way down the hall and then stopped. Bass was back on the phone. "Great. Okay. Can you . . . ? Right." To me: "There's a keypad on it, all letters no numbers, and a display screen with nine flashing *X*s. We need nine letters."

Nine letters could be anything. Nine numbers would have given me more to go on, but letters could be just words. Oscar could crack it, but my laptop would have to be connected to the detonator for it to run through all the possible combinations of letters. There wouldn't be time to go get my laptop where I assumed it was, lying in Jonas's bag next to his body, and then log in and then train someone over the phone to run it.

Bass was totally calm. "Let's take this really simply. This is a game to him. The letters won't be random—they'd have to have meant something to him. And they could be simple because he never thought you'd be able to communicate with anyone. He could have made it really obvious."

"Kill Digit." Ella was counting on her fingers. "That's nine letters. And it's what he wanted to do."

"Try it." Bass addressed the waiting police officer who was presumably just sitting there watching the clock tick away on our lives. "Try 'Kill Digit.' Yes, I'm serious. Try it. Please." We waited and watched the red blinking lights on the window, hoping for a change. "No? Okay, stay on the line."

Clarke was visibly agitated. "What else have we got? What else do you know about him? His dog's name? Who wrote *Silent Spring*?"

"It's not nine letters. His Wi-Fi password was FurnisFire—that's ten." My mind was racing through every conversation I'd ever had with him. Bass was right. He would have given me a clue, some sort of a chance. Otherwise it just wasn't fun for him. All these codes of his that I'd cracked in the past were just codes for their own sake. He could have just come on out with the information: *Pssst, go blow up the Tree of Life at Disney World*. He took some sort of pleasure in making the people around him work for information.

When we were down to fifteen minutes, the police officer (whose name I still don't know) spoke up. "Listen, guys, I can only stay for another ten minutes, then I'm going to have to get me and this dog out of here."

"Thank you." Bass was totally resigned to his fate.

I had no reason not to get onboard. "You guys, I'm really sorry to have brought you all into this. And not to be able to get you out of it. I've been playing this game with Jonas Furnis for seven months. He's dead, and we're going to be too. I . . . I don't even know who won."

"Pretty much looks like he did, Digit." Clarke was angry, and I didn't blame her at all.

Scott was busy reassembling Clementine. It was like watching a mortician make up a dead body. Well, I assumed that's what it would be like. I mean, gross.

Bass took my hand. It was too late for this to seem like romance. I was just a person to grab on to as we watched the clock tick down. We had five minutes less than we thought we did, since the officer was smart enough not to want to stay in the building till the end. "He didn't know he was going to die. But he knew he was going to win." I could picture Jonas

Furnis walking out the door. And there it was: "Checkmate! Officer, try it. Checkmate."

I held my breath and squeezed Bass's hand. From the phone in the middle of the room, we heard, "Got it!" and the lights on the windows and door went green.

Bass and I held on to each other in relief for anywhere between thirty seconds and a week. It was hard to tell. When I finally looked up, Tiki was standing over us with her arms folded, shaking her head. "Girl. Something's on here. Don't lie to me." I hugged her and the shell-shocked hackers.

I handed Clementine's phone to Scott. "Thank you," I said to both of them.

Clarke offered a status report on my life. "Well, the good news is that your family is coming in about an hour and you're going on trial tomorrow morning. Maybe you skip the rest of your homework?"

I DIDN'T DO IT. AND I'LL NEVER DO IT AGAIN

MY PARENTS WERE WEIRD. WELL, EVERYTHING was a little weird, me included. The entire incident with the bombs had taken place while they were flying, so when the police gave me my phone back, I sent them a text:

> Some crazy stuff happened at MIT, but I'm fine. See you soon.

I'm guessing this softened the blow when they pulled up at campus to find my dorm completely surrounded by police cars and the press. The police had confiscated the bombing devices that were on my windows and door and had taken all of our statements. We watched as an ambulance took Jonas Furnis's body away. Bass insisted that I stay inside my room while he went out and announced to the media that I had saved the lives of everyone in the dorm and had no comment for them at this time. Watching him handle the jungle of cameras and microphones, I could easily imagine Bass out in the world.

When Bass came back up to my room, we were all sitting where he'd left us. What had just been the least safe place in the world now seemed like the only safe place. Bass sat down next to me and put his arm around me. "I can see why maybe you need a break from all this."

"Makes jail seem kinda relaxing, right?"

My parents knocked on the door and we all jumped. Bass opened the door and said hello. My mom gave him a hug and a kiss, which seemed way inappropriate, and my dad shook his hand.

My mom grabbed me. "Darling! The police told us what happened. Are you all right?"

Clarke answered for me. "She's all right. She's used to this. But I nearly had a heart attack. I've got to get in shape for this lifestyle."

I hugged my parents. "Yeah, well I'm done with this lifestyle. Jonas Furnis is dead, his games are over, and I've cracked my last code. I'm starting a whole new boring life, dedicated to stuff normal people do . . ."

Ella reminded me, "As soon as you get out of jail."

"It's going to be her honor to go to jail. She stuck it to the Man . . ." Clarke said as she led Ella and Scott out of the room. She seemed to have a renewed sense of enthusiasm now that she remembered I was going to be martyred.

Tiki was in her own room, right where she was supposed to be, and I guess Bass realized he was the only one out of place. "I guess I should give Buddy that walk now. I'll see you tomorrow in court, okay?"

"Thanks." We both stood there, stuck again.

Luckily my dad was hungry. "Let's get going back to the hotel to meet your uncle Bob for dinner. Tiki? Bass? Would you care to join us?" They both declined.

We caught up over a perfectly ordinary dinner. It turned out Danny hadn't come because he'd gotten an audition for a starring role in a new series on the Disney Channel. "Are you joking? He had the idea to become an actor like two and a half weeks ago, and now he's going to be the star of his own series?" I was surprised but not really that surprised. You have to remember that Danny has a Fast Pass to anywhere he wants to go.

My dad said, "He told me to tell you, 'Go big or go home.'"

"I'm thinking about going small and staying home from now on."

"If that's your choice. Now, Bob, do you have anything to discuss with Digit before tomorrow? Are you all set?"

Uncle Bob was twirling spaghetti around his fork with more concentration than he'd shown my case. "All set."

"Well, all set how? I mean, I'm pleading guilty, and you have a couple character witnesses, right? Is that it?"

"That's it. The plea is actually no contest, but there's another, fancier way to say it. I'll look it up later. It means that we don't have to bother with a jury. We'll just go in with our witnesses and hope the judge goes easy on the sentencing."

Why did I wish, more than anything at that moment, that I had an attorney who didn't have to look up the fancy term for 'no contest'? Like maybe there was an attorney out there who had fancy terms rolling off his tongue all the time, rather than spaghetti on his chin.

"Now, darling, I brought a little cardigan for you to wear over your navy dress. I thought, what if there's a chill in the courtroom? Or what if a sleeveless dress shows just a tiny too much skin in that setting when all the men are going to be in suits? I'm wearing a suit myself. The one I wore when I played the district attorney in *Trial of Love*. Remember? The skirt with the little kick pleat in the back?"

"I do not remember a kick pleat." It was hard for me to imagine what I would act like the night before my teenage daughter was going to prison, but it wasn't this.

After dinner we hung out in the hotel bar for a bit. My parents were on California time, and I wasn't in any hurry to get to bed and wake up and relinquish my freedom. My dad drank a Scotch on the rocks, which was unusual but not unprecedented. He got a little tipsy.

"I couldn't be happier that Jonas Furnis is gone. Really gone," he said.

"Me too. I mean, because he was horrible. But so much of what he said sort of stays with me. It's like if he had been twenty percent less crazy, he could have changed the world."

"Well, you're the one who's still alive, and you are going to change the world. Unless you decide not to. I'm one hundred percent behind you whatever you do. Just remember I said that."

"I guess I'll have a long time to think about what I'm going to do. Prison time and then the rest of college. I think I'm probably a little burned out from all that's happened, but I wouldn't mind making my life a little more normal. And smaller."

"Good luck with that, Digit." He started to laugh, and my mom rolled her eyes at him like he was being silly.

"I'm serious."

"I'm sorry, sweetheart." Dad took off his glasses and wiped them clean (they're real; he needs them to see). "Normal? Maybe. Maybe later. But small? I think the ship has sailed on you ever having a small life."

I'M NOT MYSELF TODAY; MAYBE I'M YOU

I'VE BEEN LET DOWN BY TV a million times. You envision what the school dance is going to be like or a homecoming football game, based on what you've seen on TV. But when you get there, there's no soundtrack, the lighting's all wrong, and no one's smiling. My trial was the opposite—it was exactly like it is on TV: the courthouse looming on top of the huge steps, the hushed lobby, the double wooden courtroom doors that make the *Law & Order* "Boom! Boom!" when you close them. Seriously, it was just like TV.

I'd texted John late Sunday night before I went to sleep.

> Google "incident at MIT." I'm fine. Jonas Furnis is dead.
> Going to sleep. See you tomorrow if you can make it.

And I turned off my phone. In the morning I turned my phone back on to JOHN BENNETT 6 TEXT MESSAGES.

> I'm so sorry I wasn't there.
> You must have been terrified.
> I'm glad he's gone.
> Can we talk, are you asleep?
> Okay, I'm leaving D.C. now, will be there tomorrow.
> Love you, of course.

I like how a series of unread texts sort of reads like a sonnet.

We ran into John and Mr. Bennett as we walked into the courtroom. Mr. Bennett gave me a quick, too quick, "Hello, Digit," and John pulled me back out into the hallway. Uncle Bob called after us that we had three minutes.

"Digit, I don't even know what to say. I'm so glad you're okay." He hugged me for half of our allotted three minutes. "Are you scared?"

"This is the least scary thing that's happened to me in the past twenty-four hours. I'm fine."

John smiled. "Okay, and this is going to be okay. I can't . . . Well, it might get weird in there. Will you just trust me?"

"Weird? What about this isn't weird?"

John gave someone behind me a nod and then leaned down and kissed me. I think I've established that I am not very good at describing a kiss. In this context, this kiss could have been an "I don't know when I'll ever have a chance again" kiss. Or even an "I'm so relieved you weren't blown up" kiss. I deserved either. But what I got was neither of those. It was more like a kiss that was put on me. Like when you have a stamper for a return address and it's almost out of ink. You press it down on the paper and hold it there, just to make the ink stay. This kiss was stamped on me. I'd never had this particular kind before, and I felt a little like a fire hydrant that had just been marked.

I turned to see Bass behind me, hands crossed over his DIG IT T-shirt and looking like he didn't really know where to be. He shook hands with John. "So today's the big day."

"It is," John replied.

"I'm pretty sure yesterday was a big day. This? We know how it's going to end." I was trying to be light, trying to make this okay for everyone. I mean, I had no one to blame but myself for all this, and I was kind of sick of everyone feeling sorry for me.

John said to Bass, "Nice T-shirt." And it sounded less like a compliment than it should have.

We entered the courtroom, and, just like on TV, there was a long table just for Uncle Bob and me. My parents and my star witnesses were seated directly behind me. John took an empty seat next to his dad in the back. All of the other seats were filled with reporters and other interested parties. *On TV don't they close these things to the press?* I had a feeling that the press was exactly who the prosecution wanted here.

Court was called to order at exactly nine a.m. The Honorable Alvin Horowitz presiding. "In the case of *The United States of America versus Farrah Higgins,* how does the defendant plead?"

Uncle Bob stood up and approached the bench. He stopped and looked at his yellow legal pad for reassurance before saying, "My client pleads nolo contendere." A big smile took over his face, like he'd just gotten down the sidewalk on a two-wheeler for the first time. Before sitting down, he explained to the judge, "That means no contest."

Opening statements were made. The prosecutor: "We have here today a very straightforward case of a very complicated crime. Miss Farrah Higgins, a student at MIT, is pleading no contest to hacking into the mainframe of the Department of Defense of the United States of America. This security breach put the lives of everyone in our nation in jeopardy. She did so willfully and with intent to take information that was not hers to take at that time." *True that.*

Uncle Bob: "Your Honor, my client is eighteen years old. She is a freshman at MIT and was trying, misguidedly, to make it to a toga party on time when she decided to hack into the DOD. She had formally requested access to the information that she took, and that access had been granted. She gained access to the DOD's systems on her own just to speed up the process. You might call it a timing difference." Uncle Bob turned to me for approval. I should have just gotten up there and given the Tater Tot defense—same difference.

"Since that time, Miss Higgins's life has been in jeopardy several times in defense of her country and the well-being of her classmates . . ."

"Objection!" I swear, exactly like on TV. "Her actions subsequent to the events in question have no bearing on the events in question . . ."

The prosecution called its first witness, a guy named Norb Wolford, whose job it was to keep the data at the DOD secure. He outlined my crime in such excruciating detail that even I was bored by it. What was interesting was what he left out. He described exactly what I did, without revealing any details about how I did it. Probably smart.

When he finished, the prosecution called its second witness. "The prosecution calls Henry Bennett to the stand." *Wait. What?* I swung around to look at him as he walked down the aisle to the witness stand. He did not meet my eye. John gave me a slow shake of the head. No? Was he shaking his head no? As in, *No, this is not really happening?* Or, *No, my dad is not really going to get up there and say anything against you?* Or, *No, you shouldn't have agreed to trust me?*

Mr. Bennett was sworn in and answered some questions about his position at the CIA. And then it began.

"Mr. Bennett, how long have you known Miss Higgins?"

"Seven months."

"In that time have you noticed anything extraordinary about her?"

"She has an extraordinary ability with numbers and codes."

"At what point did you realize that she was a danger to society?"

"Objection!" I bellowed.

"Miss Higgins, please. I repeat: At what point did you realize that she was a danger to society?"

"I knew Miss Higgins for less than a week when I realized that her gifts could be used as a weapon."

"Would you call her a threat to national security?"

"I think she's demonstrated that on her own."

"So at what point did you begin tracking her computer activities in the interest of protecting state secrets?"

I passed a note to Uncle Bob: *It was illegal surveillance.*

Uncle Bob shouted, "Objection! Mr. Bennett's surveillance of my client's laptop was illegal. None of this testimony should be admitted." *Take that!*

"Your Honor, I submit Exhibit A, an unlimited warrant to monitor Miss Higgins's telecommunications and computer activity, signed by the director of the CIA, July 19 of this year."

Uncle Bob sat down and shrugged.

"In your surveillance, when you saw that Miss Higgins hacked into the DOD, what was your reaction?"

"I realized that she was more dangerous than I thought."

With that, the prosecution rested its case.

I watched Mr. Bennett walk back down the aisle, trying to catch his eye for some sort of clue that maybe I'd been *Punk'd*. I turned to look at John and got that same stupid shake of the head. This had to be a joke or a mistake—or maybe, most likely, I was having a nervous breakdown and imagining this whole thing. I mean, the kidnapping and then the whole almost-being-blown-up thing? It can take a toll.

I turned to my parents and saw this: Mom was looking into a compact and applying a thin layer of lip gloss. Dad was looking at me, nearly expressionless. Not expressionless like disbelief or shock that is so extreme that you can't muster up any expression. More expressionless like you're watching the third hour in a row of NASCAR racing on TV.

The only confirmation I had that this had actually happened was from Uncle Bob. "I can't believe he just did that to us. I ate his bacon."

"If the defense would please call its first witness . . ."

Uncle Bob was stunned for sure and didn't seem like he was quite ready to proceed. The plan was that I was not to testify on my own behalf, because if the prosecution started asking me questions and I seemed too knowledgeable about these things, I might freak out the judge. My job was to sit there in my nice navy dress and look young and unthreatening. Mr. Bennett had taken the whole concept of my being unthreatening with him when he left.

"The defense calls Isabella Clarke to the stand." Clarke walked up to the witness stand in her now signature FREE DIGIT T-shirt and plaid pajama bottoms. Uncle Bob had suggested that she remove some of her piercings for the trial. Her face on that witness stand indicated that she did not hear that suggestion.

"Miss Clarke, please tell the court how you know Miss Higgins."

"Digit lives on my hall at MIT. She is a hero and a patriot. She is the voice of hackers everywhere who want to show the world its weaknesses. Just because you are all embarrassed that she could get into the DOD doesn't mean she needs to be treated like a hardened criminal. I say you end this thing right now, go back to Washington, and build a monument to her . . ."

Established so far: Dangerous girl has crazy friend. This trial wasn't going quite my way.

Uncle Bob knew when to cut his losses. "Thank you, Miss Clarke. You are excused. The defense calls its final witness, Mr. Sebastian Taylor, to the stand."

Bass was sworn in and sat down. He looked unusually agitated.

"Before we begin, Mr. Taylor, are you a hacker?"

"I am not."

"Good." There were chuckles in the courtroom, which I found a tad bit insensitive.

"Would you please tell the court how you know my client?"

"I am her RA, residential adviser, on her hall in McKinsey at MIT."

"Would you consider her a threat to society?"

"No."

"Would you please share with the court what you know of her character?"

"Her character? This whole thing is crazy! Do any of you people have televisions? She saved my life yesterday. Isn't that enough?"

"Objection!" the prosecutor shouted.

"If you would please stick to her personal traits and qualities," Uncle Bob reminded him.

"Fine. My dog loves her. She can't dance. She looks away from you when she's about to say something she means. And she only looks at you if you're talking to someone else. She doesn't mind silence, but she'll open up to you if you're on a walk. Sure, she's a genius. But not this threatening genius she's being made out to be. More than anything, she wants to fix things. Make them better."

He stopped talking, like maybe he couldn't believe he'd said so much.

"So you would vouch for her character?"

"Of course. This is ridiculous. I'd do anything for her."

Bass looked at me, no smile. I smiled a thank-you. I saw him look to the back of the courtroom. I turned around and saw John leaning back in his seat, arms crossed and eyebrows all the way up. *Really? You're pissed that this guy's my friend? Can we talk about your dad for a sec?*

I looked away from both of them. I had bigger problems for sure because just then Uncle Bob announced, "The defense rests."

The court went into recess so that the judge could decide my fate. My dad hugged me. "It's going to be okay." *Would everybody please stop saying that?*

"Dad, how could it possibly be okay? I was pretty sure I was going to jail already. But how could Mr. Bennett have done that to me?"

"He was just doing his job, honey." *Et tu, Daddy?*

Bass was waiting behind my dad. "Hey."

"Hey, thanks."

"You've been completely screwed over."

"Feels like it."

"Where'd the boyfriend go anyway?" Bass was angry. And that made him seem like the only sane person in the room. I looked around the crowd, and John was gone.

I said, "He wouldn't leave. Nothing's making sense to me right now." Bass hugged me. I started to cry. "I really feel like I'm going crazy."

Bass turned my face up to his. "Listen, you're probably going to jail, probably for not that long. And I'm going to come visit you. And I'll bring research for you to read. I'll bring Buddy if they'll let me. He's going to miss you."

Judge Horowitz banged his gavel. "Welcome back to the speed-dating version of the criminal justice system . . ." Chuckles all around. *What?* "This case has been quite literally open and shut, and the penalty seems quite straightforward as well. I hereby sentence Miss Farrah Higgins to three months in minimum security prison in Duluth, Minnesota. Miss Higgins, if you would please go with the bailiff . . ."

I stood up and hugged Uncle Bob. "Three months is not the end of the world, Digit. You'll be back at school before spring break." *Ever heard the expression "Easy for you to say"?*

I hugged my unsurprised parents. "What's with you guys?"

My mom said, "Henry told us it would be about three months. We were expecting this. Just three months, darling, and you'll be back at school." She snapped her fingers to show me just how fast three months' incarceration can seem. *Hello, I'm going to jail now.*

Dad was a little more earnest. "Honey, you are going to be fine. I know it. I promise. And I am very, very proud of you. You have no idea."

MY CHILD WAS INMATE OF THE
MONTH AT THE COUNTY JAIL

WHEN THEY PUT ME IN THE van to take me to the airport, there were a few things I was wondering in the back of my mind: *Why are they going to the trouble to fly me somewhere? Isn't there a suitable prison within driving distance? Why do they never show this part of the process on TV?* Usually the perp (now felon) just leaves the courtroom, looking over his shoulder. After the commercial, he's behind bars. I was in some sort of criminal justice purgatory that I wasn't familiar with.

In the front of my mind, I was wondering: *What sort of food do they serve in jail for Thanksgiving? When are they going to give me my orange jumpsuit, before the flight or after? Will I have to sit in the cargo area like in* Con Air? *Is John really letting me go to jail without saying goodbye to me? What was that kiss about? Could this be because he thinks there's something going on with Bass? Is there something going on with Bass?* Let's face it. I was a girl who could use three months in a jumpsuit just to sort things through.

We drove out of Cambridge and into a more rural area. I saw a small airport building, a landing strip, and a few airplane hangars. *Am I too dangerous to take to Logan Airport now that I'm a threat to national security?* I was starting to get mad all over again when we stopped outside of an airplane hangar. The driver came around to let me out of the van, like a limo driver would, except he had to since these doors did not open from the inside.

He led me to the door of the hangar and said, "Please wait here." *Convicted felon here! You're going to let me just hang out alone? How could I be a threat to the public* and *a low flight risk?*

And then the craziest possible thing happened. He came back out, accompanied by Mr. Bennett, John, and the director of the CIA.

My mouth dropped open and a machine-gun fire of questions came out, at all of them and no one in particular. "What's going on? How could you have said those things about me? How could you have been saying you were tracking me to protect me when you were tracking me to arrest me? It's called entrapment. I watch TV, I know! And you, how could you have left? How could you have let him do this? What the hell is going on here?"

I wanted answers and I got silence, as they all kind of looked at each other to see who was going to start.

"I'm waiting."

"I've heard." Mr. Bennett gave me a little smirk.

"Dad . . ." John managed to make the word last for two syllables.

"Digit, remember when we were in my living room and you were going through Jonas Furnis's bank statements with me? I knew then that the CIA needed you. More than science needs you, more than my love-struck son needs you. I also knew that you'd never come voluntarily. You have a sort of creative curiosity that would not naturally lead you to law enforcement. So I started tracking your laptop, in part to make sure you were okay, but also in the hope that you'd do something stupid that I could use as a bargaining tool."

"And you did. Something stupid, that is." The director seemed to think he was helping.

I turned to John. "And you knew about this?"

"Not until Saturday."

"We don't have a lot of time, and we have a deal for you."

"Whatever it is, I'd rather go to jail."

Mr. Bennett softened. "I had to say those things in court because I had to make sure you got jail time. The judge had orders to give you exactly three months, but he refused to deliver the sentence unless I could convince the press that you were dangerous." *And I'm the criminal here?* "We need you for one more job. The public thinks you're in jail, but it will never turn up on your record. We just need you to come with us for three months."

"My parents are going to visit me in prison. Are the guards just going to tell them I'm in the shower?"

"I ran this all by your dad in Virginia. They know. I think he's secretly proud of how much you can help your country. And it's only three months, maybe two. You'll be back in school, and we'll leave you alone."

I turned to John. "And you?"

"I will not leave you alone."

"I mean, you're buying into with this insanity?"

"Dad, Uncle Jim. Can we just have a second?" John pulled me to the side for the illusion of privacy.

The director rolled his eyes. Mr. Bennett told him, "You're going to have to get used to this. It's nuts with these two."

"Digit, you were guilty anyway. And I'm not going to let you go to prison if I can help it. I'm working for the CIA now. And we really do need you on this. We can be together, like normal people, and then you can go back to school. And keeping you away from that RA for a few months is just a bonus."

I think I was supposed to say something here. Something like *Oh, don't be silly!* Or *Who? That guy?* But I let it drop.

"C'mon. It's this or jail. And you're going to love this project. It's right up your alley. No bombs, just numbers. This is the sort of thing you were born for. Your destiny."

Mr. Bennett and the director were on us again. "What's it going to be, Digit?"

"I am so sick of you people acting like you know what my

purpose in life is and telling me how I need to crack some code to stop some psycho. Is 'I don't want this' impossible for you to understand? I will happily get back in that van and go to jail."

The director answered his phone and hung up quickly. "The president wants to leave. Now."

"Who?" As I asked, a huge aircraft pulled out of the hangar and stopped a hundred feet from us. The door opened as a truck towed the access stairs over to it.

John turned me to face him. "Just say yes, Digit. Please."

The director held an imaginary clipboard. "One and done, Digit. One and done."

Without answering, I started walking with them toward the plane. It said UNITED STATES OF AMERICA along the side and had a highly stylized symbol by the door, maybe the biggest bumper sticker I've ever seen. I stopped at the bottom of the stairs, finally able to read it: SEAL OF THE PRESIDENT OF THE UNITED STATES.

I turned to John. "Is this Air Force One?"

"Yep."

The director: "The president is waiting. Hustle up."

Mr. Bennett stood next to me as I looked up the stairs. "Come on. One job working for me, then I'll be your pal or your mentor or your father-in-law. Whatever you want. But we need you. You just might learn something."

I thought of Danny. *Go big or go home.*

John held his hand out to me as if to lead me up the steps. *Steps? I need help with steps now? Maybe when we got onboard, he could help strap me into my booster seat and bring me a juice box.* If I was going to go enlighten the president with my newly gained nano-knowledge and help the country with whatever numbers problem he had, I was going to do it on my own.

Looking at John's outstretched hand, I made my decision. I put my hands deep in my pockets and walked up the stairs to board the plane.

ACKNOWLEDGMENTS

I can barely scratch the surface of my gratitude. Thank you to my agent, Helen Breitwieser, who has taken Digit places I never dreamed she'd go. A special thank-you to my editor Julia Richardson for her devotion to Danny and for reminding me about what ruined the magic of Sam and Diane. I'm starting a new book today, mainly because I like hanging out with you.

Thank you to the people of Rye, New York, who generously offer their talents to others and, so frequently, to me. Just to name a few: Elaine Kaman Tibbals for photographing me, Jane Rosenstadt for explaining the legal mumbo jumbo, Lynn Halpern for getting the word out, Robin and Peter Jovanovich for keeping my pen moving, and Lee Woodruff for opening doors.

Thank you to the very, very smart John Carls— Digit enthusiast, and mentor and friend.

Thank you to my young (and just young-looking) readers: Gretel Dennis, Natalie Wilson, and Stefanie Wilson. Your insights are so good that I'm worried you may stop working for free. And to my peeps Tom, Dain, Tommy, and Quinn: Thanks for making me laugh every single day. You are behind every story that I tell.